M000074865

SHADES OF VICTORY

The Off The Grid Survivor Book 4

CONNOR MCCOY

Copyright © 2018 by Connor McCoy

All rights reserved.

No part of this book may be reproduced in any form or by any electronic or mechanical means, including information storage and retrieval systems, without written permission from the author, except for the use of brief quotations in a book review.

CHAPTER ONE

"OVER HERE!" shouted the doctor as the three adults behind him helped the wounded lady through the house to the living room. Like most doctors, Doctor Ronald Darber understood that time was of the essence for any life-threatening injury. It was doubly important when the wounded person also happened to be pregnant.

Darber yanked open the couch, unfolding the bed tucked inside, just in time for Carla Emmet to be placed on top of it. She yelped in pain as she was laid down. Darber instantly reached for his bag. He had tucked it away by the couch before he joined the fight for this homestead. He couldn't haul around this medicine bag in the middle of a gun battle, but he always knew where it would be and could grab it if needed.

A gun battle. That was the last thing Ron Darber

had expected to wind up involved in. But the times had changed, and this small town doctor now was a battlefield medic.

Sarah Sandoval applied pressure on the bleeding wound with a folded cloth. Darber quickly fished for his tools. Antiseptic was needed. A bullet penetrating the skin could wreak all sorts of havoc inside the body and had to be dealt with. However, calamity also could result from the wound becoming infected. Cleansing the wound was a top priority.

Darber placed the open bag on the small end table by the couch. As he slid on a pair of plastic blue gloves, he couldn't help but recall the prime reason Carla was shot. It was all on his account.

This ranch, lying just off State Road 22, was viciously assaulted by a man named Kurt Marsh. The madman ruled the town of Davies with an iron fist, and detested the idea of anyone leaving his employ, especially Ronald Darber, Kurt's own personal doctor. To Kurt, the townspeople were his to do with as he wished. For the crime of defecting to Conrad Drake's homestead, Kurt vowed there would be blood. But Darber had not informed Conrad of Kurt's despotic reign in Davies. Only when a trio of Kurt's men arrived on Conrad's doorstep did the truth come out.

As Darber worked, he prayed hard that his omission did not lead to loss of life. No, he couldn't think about that happening. There was no time for self-loathing with two lives at risk.

With the bottle of antiseptic now on the small

table, Darber fished out a pair of tweezers. They were sanitized. Darber made sure of it before he packed them away. "Tom, boil me some water. Sarah, get the antiseptic ready." Then he leaned over Carla. "Carla, this is going to hurt mightily, but I have no choice. Sedation's out of the question, so you're going to definitely feel this."

Tears streamed down the young woman's face. She struggled just to spit out her words. "Just...do it...for my baby."

Darber vowed to work fast. The longer this lasted, the weaker Carla would get. Soon she might not be in any condition to handle surgery as hasty as this.

Beside her, Liam grasped her hand. "I'm here, baby," he said.

"Hold her tight." Darber would delay no longer. He inserted the tools into the wound and probed for the bullet.

Carla screamed loud and hard.

Darber gritted his teeth, ignoring the screams as he worked. As if by a miracle, he successfully extracted a small piece of metal from Carla's body. It was definitely the bullet, and to Darber's great relief, it had not shattered inside Carla. That meant there were no remaining metal fragments inside of her. At least he hoped not. Without an X-ray machine to work with, he possessed no sure way to locate bullet fragments in a human body.

"Now we clean the wound and bind it," Darber said. "Sarah, pour on the antiseptic!"

Sarah opened the bottle and administered the liquid. Carla cried out even more. Liam held her tightly. "Don't worry, baby. You're going to make it. You're going to make it."

Carla let out a loud cry. Sarah, who was also Liam's mother, fought back tears. Darber didn't know her well, but imagined the lady, a former suburbanite who fled to this ranch after being imprisoned in her home town by a ruthless warlord, was having a hard time weathering this crisis. Tom, who had returned with the water, put up a braver front.

"We all came from different worlds before this," Darber thought. Tom was a computer consultant. Sarah was his girlfriend. Liam and Carla were college students. And Darber was a doctor in a small town.

Then their whole world turned upside down when a flare from the sun struck the Earth's atmosphere and fried all unprotected electronics with an electromagnetic pulse. Cars and trucks came to sudden stops on the road. Computers went dark, never to be lit up again. Refrigerators and freezers stopped working, their contents spoiling within hours. The whole modern infrastructure of the United States, and perhaps the whole world, was shut down, throwing humankind backward in time a few hundred years. Now food, water, shelter, even security, were things to be fought for day by day.

Just now, they had taken up arms to preserve those things for this countryside homestead.

Darber fought the urge to cringe, to step back. Carla's cries would not rattle him. He would see this through to the end.

———

LYING BACK in the easy chair across from the couch, Ron Darber let out a long breath. Sweat dripped down his face. Carla lay still on the sofa. Her screams of pain had given way to moans, which in turn surrendered to quiet groans and coughs. Her eyes were mostly closed, only occasionally opening a little more to look around.

"She..." Darber caught himself from tilting over. "I think we've successfully stabilized her." He wasn't even sure who he was talking to anymore. The exhaustion of the past several hours had caught up with him. "Stopped the bleeding...early. Wound wasn't big. That maybe made...the difference." He gripped the chair to keep steady.

"Water." Conrad spoke up.

Darber turned around, sighting Conrad and Camilla. They probably never had left the room since their arrival. Liam was also still in the room, on the other side of the couch, leaning over Carla. He had been with her in some way since helping her into the room.

"What?" Camilla blinked her eyes as if coming out of a daze.

It was then that Darber noticed the red-stained cloth tied around her right shoulder. Conrad himself had bound up his left arm with a small piece of cloth that, once blue, now appeared dark reddish. The two of them obviously had suffered wounds in their ordeal. Given their older ages—Conrad at 60, Camilla at 51—Darber was doubly concerned. He could not delay in checking their wounds.

"We need to get Ron some water," Conrad said. Usually the old rancher who owned this homestead was energetic, sharp and quick, but after today's ordeal he was tired and moved with a bit of a jerk in his step.

"Never mind." He turned to the kitchen door. "I'll do it myself."

But before he could push past the doorframe, he was blocked by Sarah and Tom. Tom clutched a handful of clean towels, while Sarah handled a pitcher of water. Slowly, Conrad stepped aside and permitted the pair into the room.

Sarah poured water into small cups, first for Darber, then for Conrad and Camilla, and finally for Liam. Liam took his drink without averting his eyes from Carla.

Darber drank quickly, cleaning out the cup in one swig. Then he turned to Conrad and Camilla. "I have to...I have to check you two out."

"Easy, Ron," Conrad said, "We'll come to you."

Conrad and Camilla knelt next to Darber. The doctor offered to get out of his chair, but Conrad refused. Darber was exhausted. He needed the seat if he was going to be effective.

"Not a bad dressing," Darber said as he looked at Camilla's gunshot wound.

"I'm starting to get the hang of this," Camilla grinned. "What's that, two times I got shot since I came here?"

"Fortunately, this one doesn't look bad. It didn't..." Darber then started coughing. He waited until he was done before continuing. "It hit the arm at an angle. Didn't penetrate deeply. Sarah, the antiseptic, please."

Sarah hurried to bring the bottle over, her graying hair brushing against Darber's balding dome. "Thank you," he said. She had calmed down in the past hour, as it became clear that Carla likely would pull through.

Then she stopped and looked at Conrad. "Kurt?" she asked softly.

"Took his own life," Conrad replied gently, "He's still out in front. I hadn't had a chance to move him. I wanted to check up on you all."

Sarah smiled a little. "I'm glad you're alright." Then she glanced at Camilla. "You too."

Camilla made a fist and pumped it very weakly. "You weren't too bad out there. You helped save us all."

"Thanks." Sarah clutched her arm. "But right now, I feel like throwing up."

Conrad turned his head to Tom, who just had finished dumping all the dirty cloths used on Carla in a pile. She already was draped in fresh towels and a blanket. "Tom," Conrad called. The younger man turned his head. "Why don't you go help out your lady? Take a break."

Tom nodded. "Sure. Let me just get these things out of the way." He picked up the soiled cloths and removed them from the room.

Darber began binding up Camilla's wound. He thought to himself, *Your lady*. Interesting for Conrad to say that, considering Sarah was once Conrad's lady. The two had divorced under less than friendly circumstances. Now Sarah had found a new love interest in Tom Richards, although their relationship had suffered a few bumps in the road since the EMP hit. But the two seemed to have patched things up and enjoyed a harmonious life together. As for Conrad, Camilla had been his on and off love interest for a while. It was hard to tell what those two were up to nowadays.

As Darber finished redressing Camilla's injury, Conrad turned his attention to his boy. "Liam, I think it's time you let Darber look at you." But Liam didn't respond.

"Liam!" Conrad called, "C'mon, we all got to get checked out."

"I'm fine," Liam said with a low growl underlying his voice.

"Liam, your face looks like it was run over by a pickup," Conrad said, "We're not ending the day without all of us getting looked over."

Liam cleared his throat. "Doc, how in the hell did Carla get out of the shelter?"

Darber looked away. He didn't want to catch the young man's eyes. "Carla is a very resourceful young lady. She was able to find the key to unlock the door."

"How?" Liam asked.

"She probably found one of my notes in the containers," Conrad said quickly, "I didn't have time to ransack them to get rid of anything that could unlock the door. I had to set the traps outside and plan the ambushes."

"But why did you have the unlock codes in there anyway?" Liam asked.

Conrad scowled. "Think about it. You really wanted me to lock someone down there without a chance of getting out? The whole point of the shelter is that it's hard to break into, not impossible to break out of. It wasn't supposed to be a prison. Sticking her down there was just improvising."

Now Liam turned to Darber. "But Doctor Ron, couldn't you have stopped her?"

"I tried," Darber said quietly. Conrad wanted him and Carla to stay down in the shelter room in the home's basement, but Carla found the override code that unlocked the vault door.

"Liam, stow it," Conrad said. "Your lady here saved your ass. From where things stand, it seemed like everything may have worked out for the best."

Liam wasn't done protesting. However, Carla's soft voice cut through the room and drew everyone's attention. "Liam...don't chew out Doctor Ron." She blinked her eyes, but could not open them fully. "I wanted to get out and help you," she whispered. "I would have slugged him if I had to."

Darber straightened up. "Well, thank God it didn't come to that."

Carla smiled. "C'mon. Don't blame him. Even that stupid gun trick didn't work."

Liam turned back to Darber. "Gun trick? What is she talking about? Did you pull a gun on Carla?"

Sarah's mouth dropped open. "Doctor!"

"Actually, that was my idea," Conrad quickly added. "Look, we'd never put Carla in any real danger. You want to get pissed at somebody? Fine. Get pissed at me. Sticking her in the shelter with Doctor Ron was my idea. I'm the man in charge of this castle, and if something went wrong, it was my call."

A fly buzzed Conrad's face. He swatted it away. Then he noticed additional flies zipping around the room. He then inhaled deeply.

Darber did as well, and then winced when his nostrils caught the foul odor. "What in God's name is that?"

Conrad looked to the door to the kitchen. "The dead," he said, "We've been tending to Carla so long that we forgot a bunch of corpses are lying in and around our home. And now they're attracting vermin." He waved his hand in front of his face. "If Carla's out of danger, we have to drag these cadavers away from the house or this place is going to stink to high heaven."

————

CLUTCHING the empty bucket in her hand, Sarah strolled out the door and into the side yard. The well was a short walk away. With Carla stabilized, they could afford to start taking water from the well again and give the shower water a rest.

Before Sarah could emerge from the shadow of the homestead, she spotted a hand draped across the grass. She gasped and tossed aside the bucket. Then, she fiddled for her gun. However, she had removed it along with her belt and holster earlier as Tom was hastily checking her for wounds. She hadn't thought to put it back on.

Sarah then realized the hand belonged to a dead man lying on the grass. He looked up, eyes closed, dried blood trailing from his lips. This man was part of Kurt's strike force. He must have been shot in the house and fled, only to expire out here. Sarah's bullet might have even been the one to kill him.

Sarah trembled, but her initial bout of fear soon turned to anger. Then, she let out a holler and slammed her boot into the dead man's abdomen.

"Damn it! Damn it! Damn it!" Sarah let out a string of expletives that she almost never used. "Why?" She looked down at the dead man's body through welling tears.

A stream of rapid footfalls caught up to her. "Sarah." Tom stopped next to her and took her arm. "Are you alright?"

Sarah didn't stop looking down at the corpse. "I... no. No, I'm not." Then she coughed before speaking again. "I just remembered we had all these bodies. I... I wonder how many times I walked by them. I didn't notice before."

"It's okay." Tom pulled Sarah closer. "We'll get rid of them. Helping Carla came first."

"Why did these sons of bitches come here? Why did they make me have to kill them?" Sarah asked as she sank her head into Tom's shoulder. "I hate this. What am I doing here, fighting for my life like something out of a war movie?"

"I know how you feel. But you helped save us, including your grandchild." Tom patted the back of her neck.

"I know. And I'd do it again. I just feel sick," Sarah replied. "I've never had to do anything like this before. I said I'd never be a victim again. It's just saying it and doing it, they're so different."

Tom sighed. "I know. It's like real life suddenly gives you the full initiation. I remember when Conrad dragged me along on the raid on Maggiano's. I never thought I'd ever do anything like that. But then the moment came, I saw you, and I knew what I had to do." He paused, deep in thought. "The moment changed me. I don't think I'd recognize myself a year ago."

"I think that's what's scary," Sarah said, "I don't want to change into a killer."

"You won't." Tom patted Sarah's back. "You won't."

CHAPTER TWO

THE ANGLE of the setting sun cast a dark shadow on the inside wall of the back porch. It seemed to fit Conrad's mood well. He sat outside in his favorite chair, on the porch that today had been a battlefield. He refused to acknowledge the fresh bullet holes, the dried blood on the floor, or the torn branches from the nearby bush. He just sat in the chair, not even rocking it. He remained still as he watched the sky fade to night. His favorite bottle of bourbon sat on the table, but he wasn't even in the mood to drink that.

They had spent the bulk of the day preparing a good dinner after treating Carla and patching up themselves. Then they made a quick check of the livestock before getting ready for bed. Fortunately, they discovered only two dead bodies in the house. The rest who made it inside, though wounded, managed to flee, only to perish from their wounds outside. Conrad had seen to it that the two corpses were tossed out of his home. He and Liam dragged all the corpses a short way from the house, but that was it. Conrad wouldn't bury them tonight, if he wanted to bury them at all.

He softly ground his teeth. *More bodies to bury*, he thought. He had done it once before with the bodies of Derrick Wellinger's men who died on his property. This time the cleanup would be bigger and more distasteful. Conrad had buried an IED in his front yard, which blew up a whole truckload of men. The corpses still lay in the wreckage, burned to crisps. All of that would have to be hauled away and disposed of.

Conrad did acquire one important prize. Kurt's party had arrived in two trucks. One of them had emerged from the battle unscathed, still sitting in the front yard. A fully functioning pickup truck was a valuable tool in today's world, though without working gas stations to refuel it, the vehicle would have to be used sparingly. Fortunately, Conrad had stored supplies of gasoline. He figured it could be used in generators or perhaps for his own truck, although the EMP from the sun rendered that moot.

That truck could be a getaway vehicle, Conrad thought. *If this shit happened a third time, if it was even worse, I could shove everyone in there and tell them to hit the road.*

Then maybe Carla wouldn't be shot again...

Conrad nearly swore, but he kept his composure. He wasn't sure at all if he had done the right thing by

locking up Carla in his basement shelter. On the one
hand, if she had stayed in there, she wouldn't have
been shot by Kurt. However, without her in the fight,
Kurt's right-hand man Hunter would have killed
Liam.

In short, Conrad was left with no easy answer to
his dilemma.

Footsteps approached behind him. That was
Camilla. Conrad didn't need to turn around to
find out.

She walked slowly. A fresh bandage adorned her
shoulder. Her eyes were half open, with little dark
spots under her eyes. The battle had taken a lot out
of her, but she wasn't complaining. She clutched a
folded up American flag in her arms. "Hello there,"
she said.

"Thought you were asleep," Conrad muttered.

"I probably should be. But the house doesn't
feel quite..." she sighed, "...like home, I guess. A
few too many bullet holes and dried blood stains
for me."

"I'll take care of it," Conrad said.

"I wasn't asking you to do that, at least not right
now. I think you've got enough to worry about
already. You always do," Camilla replied.

"Look, if you want a place to sleep, what about
the inside of that truck we got from Kurt?" Conrad
asked.

"Really? Sure, I think that would work." Camilla
smiled, faintly. "Maybe you can join me for a nice

night in the truck, turn on the radio, and maybe turn on the air conditioner?"

Conrad didn't turn his head. "You know you'll get nothing but static on the radio. Nobody's transmitting anymore."

Camilla chortled. "Well, thanks for poking a hole in my fantasy."

Conrad bit his lip. "Sorry, Cammie, but right now it's hard to think of being merry."

Camilla put the flag on the table, then started unfolding it. "I was thinking of raising this outside, but I figured you might need this more than the house. Besides, it's not like you're running low on flags around here."

"Thanks to you," Conrad said.

Camilla chuckled. "A few extras, Conrad. You always had the Stars and Stripes in mind around here." She had finished unfurling the fabric and now was holding it out in front of her.

"Here." She began draping it over Conrad's shoulders. "Old Glory may be just what you need to help you heal."

Gently, Conrad took the cloth and pulled it over his chest like a blanket. "Thanks," he said, softly.

After a short time relaxing in the chair, Conrad turned his head to his right. Liam strolled past an open window.

"Third time I've seen your son walk by there." Camilla turned around to face the house. "He's circling us like a falcon. He must want to talk to you."

She sighed. "I guess I'm taking too much of your time."

"That's a bunch of bull. You're fine," Conrad said, "He wants to talk to me, well, he can wait his turn."

Camilla shook her head. "No, I think that young man needs his father." She blew a slow breath from her lips. "Don't forget he didn't have you for almost thirty years of his life. If that bullet that hit you was just a few inches closer to your heart or lungs, he might have lost you for good."

Conrad nodded once. "Alright." The worst part of his divorce from Sarah was losing contact with his only son. Conrad never saw Liam mature from a child to a teenager and finally to a young man. Camilla was right.

About two minutes later, once Camilla had left the porch, Liam walked through the door, quite slowly. The young man usually approached quickly with his head high, ready to say whatever was on his mind. Tonight, his slow movements reminded Conrad of how a child would approach a distant and stern father. It was enough to melt Conrad's sour mood.

"Liam, pick up the pace. There's still some more bourbon waiting for you. It's a party of two tonight."

Liam didn't smile, but he walked a little faster. "Thanks." He sat on the chair, apart from his father.

Conrad reached for an empty glass on the table. He had brought out a pair of glasses in case company showed up. He poured some bourbon into one empty glass. "So, what's got you up at this hour? I figured you'd have been catching forty winks with what happened today."

"No, I can't sleep," Liam replied.

"Worried about Carla," Conrad said.

"She was awake and talking when I left her. Doctor Ron's staying by her side. I don't know. I think I'm just worried about..." Liam gazed up at the stars. "...what's coming next."

"I have a feeling things will turn quiet for the moment," Conrad said.

Liam raised his hands. "You don't think fifty masked goons are going to show up to avenge the great 'Kurt the Phoenix?'"

"No, I don't think that'll happen. You see, a lot of people have this thing called a self-preservation instinct. If you find out that about twenty guys with guns got their asses handed to them, odds are you're going to cross that place off as your next vacation spot." Conrad pushed down his finger as if he was crossing off an imaginary list. "You get my drift?"

"Yeah, don't mess with Conrad Drake." Liam chuckled. "I can't believe you actually put land mines in the front of the house."

"Well, the tank was in the shop, so what's an old rancher to do?" Conrad asked. Then he drank some more bourbon without skipping a beat. "Still, there's no way we can have the homestead be that exposed again. I had to work fast before Kurt showed up, so I couldn't put up all the barriers around the house that

I wanted. But now that we have some time, I can fall
some trees onto the driveway. It won't matter if some
lunatic shows up with trucks again, they won't get
near the house."

Liam sighed. "Amazing we have to do all this just
to stay alive. Do you think it's ever going to get
better? I guess what I'm trying to ask is, you think
the country's ever going to be put back together?"

Conrad drank again before answering. "It'll never
be like it was. Right now, we're in a state of anarchy.
No one's calling the shots. But I could see that
changing." The old rancher wiped his lips with the
back of his hand. "That's what I'm worried about.
Without the rule of law, power can flow into the
hands of people who just have more guns than
everyone else. Too many times, people like that are
only out for their own interests. If you can't defend
yourself, you become a serf."

Liam took a swig of his own glass. "That's, that's
real comforting."

Conrad chuckled. "No kidding. But, who knows?
The future's not written in stone. Sometimes we can
be better than what we are. Don't forget that
Maggiano, Derrick and Kurt are all dead, and we're
still here. Sometimes the bad guys don't actually win
after all."

The conversation continued for a short while.
Speaking with his son helped lift Conrad's spirits.
Still, even as they shared a final drink before Liam
left to go back inside, that question of the future still

nagged at him. Conrad knew he was going to be even busier than usual for the next few days.

———

As LIAM LEFT HIS FATHER, he thought back to all the effort his dad had put into protecting the homestead. It was astonishing. The way his dad had devised the placement of the bombs in the gravel before Kurt's men showed up seemed like something out of an action movie. The strategy of boxing in most of Kurt's strike force inside the house was also a marvel. Instead of allowing the invaders to fan out across the property, where they could conceal themselves behind trees or in tall grass, Conrad decided to let Kurt's men get what they came for, and let the home be their tomb.

But despite Liam's amazement, just looking at his dad sitting in that chair reminded the younger man of his dad's years of isolation. He should have spent the past few decades with his family, not cooped up here preparing for whatever catastrophe he feared would come. It was like his father was serving a long prison sentence. True, his dad now would spend his last years with his family, but it never could make up for lost time. To Liam's great disappointment, he almost never would recall his father as a younger man, never remember what it was like to grow up with him, and to see him grow older gradually with the years.

He wandered through the open doorway to the

bedroom he shared with Carla, creeping quietly, so as to not disturb his lady. She was lying in bed, her head tilted away from him, exposing her head of short brown hair with curls at the ends. Liam was about to step back out when she suddenly turned toward him, fully awake.

"Hey," she said with a soft smile.

"Hey," Liam repeated, "So, how's it going?"

"Aches." Carla raised her left arm and gestured to her bullet wound. "But better. It's not as bad anymore."

"That's great." Liam let out a long sigh. "Look, if you need anything to drink or eat, just call me."

"Liam, don't worry. Doctor Ron is keeping watch. You need to get some rest."

Liam rubbed his face. "I know I should. I feel like I'm going to collapse." He turned to the door. "I got to use the bathroom. I'll check back on you one more time before I crash on the couch."

He turned, but Carla's voice stopped him in his tracks. "Liam?"

Liam pivoted back to Carla. "Yeah?"

"Are you..." Carla shifted a little in the bed. "Are you mad that I broke out of the basement, came after you and all?"

Liam's eyes widened a little. "Mad at you? No."

"I know you wanted to protect me. I'm sure the last thing you wanted was me showing up in the middle of a gunfight."

"Yeah, but Dad was right. You did save my life. If

it wasn't for you, I wouldn't be here at all. I guess I feel bad that I couldn't guard the house and keep you from getting hurt."

"I don't think it'll ever be that easy for us. Maybe we're always going to put our necks on the line just to keep the world working," Carla said.

Liam yawned. "Yeah." It wasn't a comforting thought, but after today Liam figured they may always have moments like this. He just hoped Dad was right and the next one wouldn't arrive for a long time.

———

CONRAD EYED the tree with a wolfish grin. He just had finished untying the rope from the top of the tree. Thanks to Kurt's truck, he didn't have to cut down a tree only from his own property. Instead, he spent the morning scouting out the nearby woods, found a particularly thick one, cut it down, and drove the truck back with the tree trunk in tow. With some additional cutting, he could divide it in two and place one behind the other.

As Conrad walked past the tree trunk to return to his home for additional cutting tools, he spotted a familiar figure pedaling down the road on a bicycle. The thin man with balding brown hair quickly slid to a stop as he approached the driveway's edge. Nigel Crane then parked his bike before rushing over to Conrad.

"Well, look at you. I apologize if I didn't get your canned supply ready, but as you may have noticed, I was unexpectedly occupied," Conrad said.

Nigel looked at the homestead. "So I had heard."

Conrad craned his neck to see around Nigel. "I guess the posse stopped off the side of the road for a piss, right?"

"No, I came alone. We had our problems in town thanks to Kurt and his men. I apologize for not bringing help..."

Conrad shook his head. "I was just ribbing you. I wouldn't ask for help, you know that. I told you, this was all on me. Fortunately, I didn't lose anybody."

"Thank God." Nigel let out a loud breath. "What happened to Kurt?"

"Dead. Actually, he killed himself. He saw he was pretty much done for unless he surrendered to my tender mercies. But he decided not to take the chance, I suppose."

"Damn." Nigel looked at the tree across the driveway. "So, I guess this is your next line of defense?"

"Can't take any more chances. Kurt had two working trucks at his disposal. I don't know what anyone else will be packing. This will block off my house, at least make it harder for anyone to approach it. They'll have to come at me on foot, and when that happens." Conrad chuckled. "Well, there's about a dozen places where I and my family can hide and pick them off."

Nigel nodded. "It's scary how well you can think

of these things, but whatever can keep you going in this day and age. It seems as though I'm thinking just as much about arming my town as I am about feeding it."

"Still got problems with crop thieves?" Conrad asked.

Nigel rubbed the right side of his forehead. "Not since Kurt pulled out."

"You said some of Derrick's men were coming around and causing trouble. Ever figure on going back to his place and checking it out? With him dead, that place could be a viper's nest for bandits."

Nigel sighed. "About Derrick's men. There is something I should share with you. I figured you have a right to know, and keeping secrets from friends isn't my forte."

Conrad nodded. "Go on, tell me."

"One of Derrick's men showed up in Hooper City, but he didn't come to steal anything. Actually, he was caught up with Kurt's men, but escaped. In fact, he wants to turn over a new leaf."

Conrad turned and looked at him. "So that fella who ran from Kurt? He was here not too long ago trying to shoot my son, Carla and Cammie."

"Yeah. That's the deal," Nigel said, "He claimed he was just looking for work and didn't expect things to go down as badly as they did. He's young, probably barely out of high school. I think he regrets what he did and wants to start a new life."

"What's his name?" Conrad asked.

"Sorry, but I'm keeping that under wraps." Nigel folded his arms. "I can tell you we have him, but I'm not spilling his name or what he looks like."

Conrad frowned. "Who knew Hooper City had a witness protection program? I guess you don't want anybody paying him a house call, if you know what I mean."

"Kurt and his men set one of our restaurants on fire. He helped us save some lives. I can't ignore that. At the very least, he's earned himself a chance." Nigel stepped a little closer to Conrad. "I owe it to you to let you know. I also owe it to him to give him sanctuary. What you do with that, well, it's up to you."

Conrad swallowed. Not exactly what he expected to hear today. He was a bit peeved, but not very much. He could understand if Derrick Wellinger had seduced some ignorant chaps with talk of prime real estate where they could live out their days. However, this fool Nigel spoke of did try to murder his son, Carla, their pregnant child, and Camilla. This would take a little time to process.

Nigel seemed to assume this was the end of the conversation, so he walked back to his bike and pulled up the kickstand. However, Conrad cut in by saying, "Nigel!"

Nigel looked over his shoulder.

"Thanks for being honest with me," Conrad said, "I appreciate that."

Nigel nodded. "Sure," he said.

CHAPTER THREE

SARAH RUBBED her right hand as she looked at the stacks of jars in the pantry. Beside her, Camilla reached out and took a jar from the top of the stack. "It makes my hands hurt just looking at them," Sarah said with a soft laugh. "I can't believe I canned all these jars."

Camilla eyed the jar of meat near her face. "Damn fine job, too." Then she gazed at Sarah rubbing her right hand. "Are you really hurting?"

"Yeah, a little bit." Sarah winced a little. "I've been getting slight pains since fall started."

Camilla nodded. "Yeah, age will do that to you. Soon as it gets cold, you start feeling aches and pains in your bones. Let's hope Carla cranks us out some kids soon so they can take over."

Sarah laughed. "The poor things. I thought when I got some grandkids that I'd be taking them out for movies and pizza, not showing them how to work a farm." She stepped back and then grasped the pantry door. "What a change this all has been."

"I'm just glad no one's showed up at our door to try killing us. Summer's been quiet. Hot as hell, but quiet. And even now, still nothing." Camilla stepped out of the way, so Sarah could shut the door. "It's a bit unnerving, actually."

"Not to me." Sarah backed up to join Camilla. "If the whole world just disappears and doesn't bother us, I don't care."

Camilla started her march down the hall with the jar in hand. "Well, thanks to your man, we have enough wood to keep us toasty even if Mother Nature shows up with a blizzard." Then she waved the jar in Sarah's face. "And, of course, we have all the fire we want to cook us some nice ham. Bacon! Pork!" She cackled.

"You love anything that comes out of a pig, don't you?" Sarah asked with a chuckle. "Me, I was a vegetarian in my early forties. I thought it was the best way to lose weight."

Camilla looked at her. "So, what happened?"

Sarah pushed on the kitchen door. "One day I said, 'What the hell' and bought myself a fat, greasy cheeseburger. I had to go up another jean size, but it was worth it."

Camilla laughed. "You know, I think you do have an wild woman inside you," she said as the pair strolled into the kitchen.

As Camilla set the jar on the counter, Sarah

looked out the window. Tom was bringing the latest load of chopped wood to the wood pile next to the house.

Camilla leaned next to her. "Somebody's buffed up over the years," she said.

Sarah nodded. Tom was wearing a checkered buttoned-up shirt. When he first put it on months ago, it hung loose from his body. Now the fabric clung more tightly to his chest and arms as his muscles grew and bulged. Months of hard work had changed Tom from the slender man that Sarah once knew from their days in Redmond. His dark hair, once short, had grown out long, now dangling from the back and sides of his head.

"You think he's smoking hot, aren't you?" Camilla asked.

"Yes," Sarah said dreamily, before she snapped out of it. "I mean, what? Camilla!"

Camilla slapped Sarah on the back. "Admit it, Tom the farmhand is looking pretty appetizing, isn't he?"

Sarah playfully batted Camilla away. "Well, he wasn't a slouch before." She leaned against the kitchen sink. "But, he does look nice." Her grin showed through her lips.

"So, are you two going to make it official?" Camilla asked.

"Official?" Sarah frowned. "We're already together."

"I mean the 'm' word. Are you going to marry him?"

Sarah's cheeks turned red. "Well, do you think that's necessary? I don't know how much more together we can be. And it's not like the local chapel is open."

"Are you kidding? I'm sure there's something available in Hooper City. Just drag out any pastor and have him say the words. I don't think God gives a damn if the pastor isn't licensed by the state to do marriages."

Sarah shuffled two steps back and forth. "Well, we never really talked about it lately. I don't know. Maybe we should." Then she cleared her throat. "Anyway, what about you and Conrad? Why don't you two tie the knot?"

Camilla crossed her arms. "What? You're finally ready to let him loose? Frolic with other ladies?"

Sarah frowned again. "Camilla..."

"Yeah, I know you two long ago went your separate ways." Camilla blew a strand of her dirty blonde hair out of her face. "Well, you know Conrad. Getting him to open up is like clawing open a can of tuna with a paper clip."

"But things are fine between you, right?" Sarah asked.

"Sure. I think they're very good." Camilla then walked over to the window. Conrad stopped to chat with Tom. "But I'd be lying if I said I'll fully understand the man."

Sarah leaned against Camilla. "I think if he has any brains, he'll know how lucky he is to have you," Sarah said. "We've got so much life behind us. I don't think we can afford to wait too much longer for things to happen."

Camilla watched Conrad leave Tom and go back into the fields. "Yeah," she said softly.

———

Liam stuck his head in Carla's bedroom. "Hey," he said, "Just checking in to see if you need anything."

Carla, seated in a chair by the bed, looked up at her man with a smile, even though her eyes were narrowed. "Except for my feet, again, I'm fine, unless you want to take me on an expensive cruise when this is over."

Darber stood beside Carla. "She's unchanged since the last four times you checked in." He exhaled, then finished with, "this past hour."

"Oh." Liam slowly backed away. "Okay. Well, you know where I am." He pointed his thumb behind him. "If you need me."

"Get out!" Carla quipped.

Liam obeyed and fled down the hall. Carla gazed down at the tub of water that soaked her feet. "Not that I have a problem with him waiting on me, but it does get a little annoying at times."

Darber chuckled. "Well, at least he is spared the drive to the hospital. Otherwise he'd be in here dangling the car keys every time you complained about some pain." The doctor gazed down at the bulge under Carla's red shirt. "When your little one arrives, it'll all be done right here under this roof."

"Oh boy." Carla bit her lip. "I'm crazy ready to pop but I'm also scared out of my wits. I mean, I've never done this before." She laughed. "Yeah, of course, I haven't. I just never thought I'd have my first baby on a farm."

"That's the way it used to be done." Darber stood over her. "We got everything we need in the bathroom. I don't think there's anything more we can do except await the arrival." The doctor then raised his forefinger. "Say, have you come up with a name?"

"Oh, I've thought about it. Kristin would be perfect for a girl. But for a boy?" Carla looked at the ceiling. "Liam is terrified of making his son Liam Junior. He just does not want his son to be called 'Junior.'" She laughed. "I'd love to name him after his dad, but maybe that's not the time now."

"Well, perhaps there's another male in your life that you admire, someone whose name you'd like to pass on," Darber said.

"There is my foster dad, Riley Emmet. I don't know." Carla grazed her swollen belly. "So, tell me, who do you want to be?" she asked.

———

CONRAD CLOSED the goat pen as Liam walked away

with the latest bucket of milk. "That'll be the last milking for a while," Conrad said.

Liam's boots crunched on the snow-covered ground. "I'm sure those goats are thinking they're glad they have long thick hair while we have to bundle up to handle the cold."

Conrad caught up with Liam, then walked with his son past the sheep pens on the way back to the home. "You remember the Pattersons next door? During winter they'd always dress up their chihuahua in a little black coat. He'd look up at us with those big eyes as if he was screaming for help. I think almost every animal now is wandering around naked, as God intended."

Liam laughed. "Yeah I do remember that. Mom brought me over to have them babysit me and that stupid dog would keep jumping up to lick my face." He shook his head. "But what always stunned me was that the Pattersons had triplets. Now that I think back, how did they handle three babies at once?"

"I don't know." Conrad slowed his pace, allowing them more time to walk toward the house.

For the past few months, he found himself spending more time outdoors than usual. For one thing, Conrad enjoyed the changing of the seasons to the cooler weather. Not only was work less stressful, but the cool air was much more relaxing and peaceful. It was like a balm to the wounds of the two major battles he had had to fight to hold on to his land and save his family.

Additionally, he didn't have to look at the bullet-riddled walls of his home. Sure, he had dug out a few bullets and patched up the holes with putty, but after running across so many, and so much other damage, he became fed up with trying to expunge his home of the damage dealt to it by Derrick Wellinger and Kurt Marsh's men.

So, he would spend his time out here instead. Among his crops, in the fields that ran along the edges of his land, there were no reminders of the hardships they all had suffered. Life proceeded quietly and without incident.

It also helped that Carla's pregnancy was progressing toward its last stages, even more quickly than Conrad had imagined. He wasn't sure how far along she had been when she first arrived here with Liam. Conrad's sole experience with pregnancy had been Sarah's with Liam. It took a while for her to show a baby bump. Conceivably, Carla could have been into her pregnancy for a month or two before Conrad had met her.

Which means any day now, my grandbaby could arrive, Conrad thought.

"Dad?"

Conrad tilted his head right. Liam, stopped in his tracks, was looking at him. "Dad?" Liam repeated. "I was asking how the Pattersons handled three babies at once."

"Oh." Conrad chuckled. "Sorry, was a little lost in the clouds. Anyway, I can't imagine. But you might have to. After all, we don't know how many buns Carla's got in the oven. You might find yourself with two or three little surprises."

Liam's face twitched. "I really, really hope you're joking."

Shaking his head, Conrad turned and laughed. He wasn't going to say anything else. He'd let Liam hang on the hook on that one.

"Hey! Hey!"

Conrad and Liam pivoted towards the home's side door. Camilla was hanging out the open door, waving to them. "Hurry! It's Carla!"

———

CONRAD AND LIAM burst into the living room, with Camilla and Sarah already there. Carla was seated in the big chair, breathing heavily. Darber, crouched next to her, held her hand until the two men arrived. "The first contraction was about six minutes ago," Darber said, "Liam, get everything ready. I don't know if this is time, but we had better prepare none-theless."

"Right, right." His heart racing, Liam sprinted to the bathroom.

He and Darber had planned to have Carla deliver here, but the tub would have to be cleaned first for Carla to sit in it. Fortunately, Liam and Darber had packed away some sponges and cleaner in a special pouch on the shelf near a set of cabinets. In minutes,

Liam went to work on the tub, scrubbing the inside as clean as he could make it.

Carla's scream rattled through the room. Liam swallowed. Carla had had some false alarms before, but she had never screamed that loud, or that soon after the last scream. Something was about to happen.

Sarah stuck her head through the door. "Sweetie," she said, "Darber says we need to move her in here soon." Liam quickly started drying out the tub. "The supplies. They're in your room, right?"

Liam didn't look behind him as he worked. "The grocery bag. By the nightstand," he said between huffs.

Sarah nodded. "I'll go get it." She turned, but then slowed her pace enough to say, "We're all ready for this. Just tell us what you need, and we'll be there for you and Carla."

Now Liam stopped. He turned and glanced over his shoulder. "Thanks, Mom."

CHAPTER FOUR

CONRAD PULLED his shirt taut again. He wished for something to take his mind off the wait. He even reached for the TV remote on the end table, then scolded himself for forgetting that his home's electronics no longer worked. As much as Conrad understood that the modern world he had lived in for decades no longer existed, he still caught himself reaching for a light switch or a remote control.

I guess it's because I'm remembering what it was like last time, Conrad thought.

About an hour had passed. Despite scattered screams from Carla, so far, he hadn't heard anything but the occasional raised voice coming from the direction of the bathroom. The contractions weren't very close together, but that could change in an instant. Conrad wasn't fearful of hearing Carla scream. He knew what was coming. In fact, he could recall the scene as clear as day, standing in that hospital room while Sarah gave birth to Liam.

It was a day of magic. Conrad never had felt happier than when holding his baby boy. The joy of that day made it seem impossible that the ensuing problems with Conrad and Sarah's marriage could have happened. Everything was wonderful then, and Conrad imagined Liam eventually would be joined by one or more siblings.

Liam, everything will change from this day forward. This will be the happiest day of your life. No, more than that. It'll be your proudest. Conrad glanced at the living room walls around him. Ordinarily, he swelled with pride when he thought of the home and farm he had built. But compared to the birth of his son, the construction of his house and the tending of his fields suddenly shrank dramatically by comparison.

Conrad glanced beside him. Sarah sat there, with Tom on the other side of her. Conrad managed a small, tired smile. "Bet you're glad you're on the outside looking in this time."

Sarah blinked her eyes. "What? Oh, sorry. I was daydreaming."

"Of Liam's birth?" Conrad asked.

Sarah nodded. "I can't believe that was so long ago, but now it comes back to me like it has been a few months. I can remember how the table felt, how everything smelled, holding my baby for the first time, hearing him cry." She drew in her arms and crossed them across her chest.

Conrad pondered reaching out to comfort her, but with Tom present, he wasn't sure what his boundaries were concerning his ex-wife. Camilla, seated across from Conrad, might not react well, although she likely would understand after a while. Fortunately, Tom scooted right up to Sarah and wrapped his arm around her, solving the dilemma for Conrad.

Sarah steadied herself as she glanced at Camilla. "What about you? You ever been around when a baby was born? Oh God, I never asked you if you have any children." She coughed. "I'm not hitting a sensitive spot, am I?"

Camilla chuckled. "No. I guess I never told you that. I miscarried twice when I lived in my home city. Wasn't married, had some relationships that didn't work out. It was part of the reason I went on the road." She drew in a long breath. "But yeah, losing those two was hard. I think there was a health issue. Damn if I can remember what it was. I just had my tubes tied and said to hell with it."

"I'm sorry," Sarah said.

Camilla scratched her left arm. "I figured the husband, two kids, dog, and a picket fence life wasn't for me." Then she glanced at Conrad. "But I'd be lying if sometimes I didn't envy what Liam and Carla have."

Conrad looked into her eyes and sensed the pain in them. Camilla hurt more than she let on. "Well, just remember you did a lot to make this moment happen."

Camilla smiled. "Thanks."

Carla's loud cry suddenly cut through the air, snapping everyone's attention to the bathroom. "It's happening," Sarah said. Tom held onto her tighter.

————

Oh God, here it comes again...

You're doing fine. I see the head.

Aaaaah!

There he is!

Oh, he's beautiful.

Have you come up with a name?

His name is Liam. Liam Michael Drake.

Conrad opened his eyes. He was lost in a world of memories. Ironically, the very screams that had lulled him into his daydream snapped him back out of it.

He looked across from him. Camilla was squirming in her seat. At times, she covered her ears. Clearly, she wasn't reacting well to Carla's cries.

Then, the screams stopped. Normal conversation resumed from the bathroom, when any conversation could be heard at all. But soon the sounds of a small baby's cry cut through the air.

"That's him!" Sarah held her hands to her face. "That's him!"

"Or her," Conrad said.

"Holy shit," Camilla said.

Conrad chuckled. "That's what Daddy said when I was born."

Camilla blushed. "I'm sorry. I'm so damn new to all this. I don't know what to expect."

Sarah leaned forward in Camilla's direction. "This was pretty fast. How long has it been?"

Camilla glanced at the timepiece on the end table. It was a small windup clock that still told the time. "Not even three hours."

"It's no surprise to me." Conrad folded his arms. "I worked the lass hard from sunup to sundown to keep her in shape. Those muscles of hers probably chucked the kid out before Doctor Ron could raise his hand to slap the babe on the behind."

"Conrad!" Sarah grabbed one of the pillows and tossed it at his chest. Conrad didn't move at all. He simply smiled at her.

Narrowing her eyes, Camilla looked at Sarah. "Bet you're glad you stopped at one. Can you imagine three or four kids with his sense of humor?"

Before Sarah could retort, Darber emerged from the hall. Sweat covered his face, but he wore a soft smile. "Everyone..." He clasped his hands together, then rubbed them. "I give you one healthy baby boy."

All of them broke out in cheers, with Conrad and Sarah the loudest. The two of them jumped up and hugged each other. They held each other, then separated, with only slight unease afterward about doing so. Sarah then turned and hugged Tom. Camilla quickly caught Conrad and hugged him in.

Once all the congratulatory embraces concluded,

Sarah was the first to ask Darber, "So how's Carla? Where's Liam?"

"Carla's fine. We moved her to the bedroom with the baby. Liam is still cleaning up in the bathroom." Darber chuckled. "I think he needs a moment."

"Oh, I want to see the baby. Wait, what's his name?" Sarah asked.

"Carla still isn't sure yet." Darber glanced behind him. "How about we wait until Liam checks in on her first."

Conrad glanced at the end table again. More waiting. "Shit, now I wish the television was working more than ever."

———

LIAM STOPPED at the doorway to his and Carla's bedroom. The door was slightly ajar. Darber stood in front of it. "Can I go in?" Liam meekly asked.

"Looks like you've mostly recovered." Darber chuckled. "Not bad for your first time."

"It was a first." Liam nodded his head. "Actually, it was a lot of firsts." Then he laughed, though still nervously.

"Well, I won't keep you any longer. She'll be very happy to see you." Darber then stepped aside, permitting Liam to push the door open and walk through.

Carla was lying in the bed, with the covers up to her chest. The small bundle Carla cradled lay still and quiet. As Liam approached, he heard the small breaths coming from the newborn.

Liam leaned over his newborn son. The baby's eyes were closed. A thin coat of dark black hair covered his scalp. He was bundled up in a soft blue blanket.

"More hair than I thought he'd have," Liam said.

Carla giggled. "Yep. My handsome little man."

Liam sat on the edge of the bed. "You two look amazing."

"Thanks to you," she smirked. "And thanks for not fainting during the birth. I really, really needed you."

"Hey, after all we've been through…" Liam made a fist, then patted his chest. "I can handle anything, even childbirth." Then he coughed.

"Although there was a little more blood than I expected." Liam leaned a little closer to his son. "Still need some time to think of a name? We don't have to do it tonight."

Carla giggled again. "Maybe we could just call him Junior until we come up with a name."

Liam narrowed his eyes. "Carla…"

"Okay, okay, I'm kidding." Carla looked back at her sleeping son. "I heard all the cheering up front. I can only imagine how your mom and dad reacted."

"Doctor Ron says they were over the moon. We're going to have to get them in here soon," Liam said.

"Hey." Carla looked back at Liam. "How about we name him 'Conrad?'"

"Conrad? You want to name him after Dad?" Liam asked.

"Sure. Without him, we wouldn't have our home. We wouldn't have a safe place to raise our baby." She flicked a soft strand of hair off her son's head. "Your dad's also a strong man, kind, decent. I haven't known too many men who are like that."

Liam smiled. "Conrad. I think that'll be perfect."

Carla looked at her baby's face. "You hear that? That's who you are. Nice to meet you, little Conrad."

———

TOM STUMBLED through the back door onto the porch. To no surprise, he discovered Conrad seated outside. No one else sat with him.

"Hey," Tom said, in a lower voice than he expected. The day's fatigue had caught up with him, yet he wanted to catch Conrad alone. Fortunately, that wasn't hard, as Conrad only turned in when everyone else did. And since Tom still was up, Conrad wouldn't head for bed just yet.

Conrad turned. A new bottle rested on the table beside him, a bottle of whiskey. The glass container still housed a lot of liquid. Conrad hadn't been drinking much.

"Almost midnight," Conrad said, "I don't usually get company this late."

"Mind if I sit down?" Tom asked.

"Sure. Go ahead." Conrad pointed to the glasses next to the bottle. "Pour yourself some."

Tom took the bottle and poured himself a glass. Conrad always brought spare glasses out here as Camilla or Liam frequently would come out here to chat with him. Tom recalled in the first few weeks how Conrad would act awkwardly just in small conversation, at least around him. Now Conrad seemed more at ease with company.

"I wanted to congratulate you again on the birth of your grandson," Tom said.

"Thanks," Conrad said.

"Did you get to see him yet?" Tom asked.

"Not yet. Carla still was a bit out of it. Darber recommended we wait until early tomorrow morning," Conrad replied.

"I feel a bit strange about it all. I'm the only person who really doesn't have a close connection to your grandchild. Even Camilla's kind of another grandma to Liam." Tom took a slight drink. "I'm not sure where I fit in. Sarah's the grandma, but I don't feel old enough to be like another grandfather." He let out a slow breath. "Hell, I don't even know what it feels like to be a father."

"Well, you're about to get a front row seat," Conrad said with a chuckle. "I didn't think you had any kids. You never talked about your family."

"No, I never had any. I did have two serious girl-friends before I met Sarah. Nothing ever happened. I don't know if it was because I was sterile, or it just

never happened. When I met Sarah, I was just enam-
ored. I didn't care that she was older than me, or
when she got old enough that having kids would be a
major problem for her." Tom gazed at his half-full
glass. "I'm very happy with Sarah, but I sometimes
wonder if I made a mistake not trying to have a
family."

Conrad poured himself a fresh glass. "There's not
much use complaining about the past. Trust me. You
only can push forward with the time you got left."

"Yeah, I know. I care about Sarah. I want to spend
the rest of my life making her happy." Tom drank
much of the rest of his whiskey. "I guess I'd like to, to
do something. Something more than just being a
ranch hand."

Conrad gave it some thought. "Well, you're doing
a fine job with the wood. How about you put that
talent to some more use? We've got plenty of firewood now. Ever thought about cutting down wood to
make things?" He turned his head in Tom's direction.
"My little grandson will need a crib and his own bed
someday."

Tom looked at his right hand. "I'm starting to get
a real feel for the wood." He laughed. "I never in a
million years thought I'd be something like a
lumberjack."

"There you go." Conrad raised his glass. "Guess
we're all learning something new."

CHAPTER FIVE

THERE WAS a knock on the door to Carla and Liam's bedroom. "Come in," she said, still a little weak, but with great cheer in her voice. Still in bed, she was holding little Conrad in her arms. The breaking dawn helped shine some light on the top of the baby's head.

The door opened, revealing Conrad and Sarah, with Liam behind them. "Well!" Conrad's voice boomed as he spoke, showing off the great pride that he was feeling. "What have we here? Hello there!"

Carla held up her child. His eyes remained closed, but he did push up his arm a little over the side of his head. "I think he's finally awake. He slept pretty well last night." She then spoke directly to the baby. "Hey. It's your grandma and grandpa! They've come to visit you!"

"He's so precious!" Sarah slid past Conrad, hovering right over the newborn. "And so handsome, too!" Then she looked over her shoulder at Liam. "That's his father in him."

Liam chuckled. "Thanks, Mom."

"Healthy little fella," Conrad said as he looked over the baby. "He does remind me a lot of Liam when we first took him home from the hospital."

Little Conrad yawned. His eyes fluttered open, but only briefly.

"So, did you finally give him a name?" Conrad asked.

Liam nodded. "Yeah, we did." He then smirked. "Carla, sweetie, you should probably tell him."

Carla laughed. "Well, Mister Conrad, I want you to meet little Conrad."

Conrad quickly looked down at the baby, then to Carla. "You named the little tyke after me?"

Carla nodded her head. "We both thought it would be perfect. This farm is truly the light in the darkness of the world. If it wasn't for you, we'd probably be living on the run out there."

"Well, I'm honored." Conrad stammered a bit, which was unusual, even for him. "Thank you, Carla." He looked behind him. "And you also, Liam."

Sarah smiled. "That's really sweet, Carla."

"Well, do you want to hold him?" Carla asked.

"Sure!" Giggling, Sarah held out her arms. "Come to Grandma, you!"

Sarah took the baby from Carla. Little Conrad responded with a series of "unhs" and a bit of squirming.

"Uh oh, I think the volcano's about to blow," Conrad said.

"Conrad," Sarah said, rolling her eyes. But then the baby let out a slight cry. Conrad nodded at her with an "I told you so" look.

The older Drake held out his arms. "Here, let me see how he likes me." He took his grandson from Sarah. Conrad gripped the baby, bracing his head. Little Conrad quieted down. He opened his eyes again, but briefly, revealing bright blue pupils.

"Well, seems he likes his grandpa," Conrad said with a laugh.

Carla sat up. "Don't worry," she said to Sarah. "He'll warm up to everyone soon. He's still fresh out the oven and trying to figure out what everything and everyone is!" She laughed.

Conrad paced back and forth near the window. His namesake remained calm, only yawning every now and then.

"Man, it's coming down out there," Liam said.

Conrad turned to the window. Indeed, there was a brisk snowfall just beyond the glass. "So, winter's definitely here," he said, "Thank God we prepared well."

True. Thanks to Tom's hard work, they had more than enough firewood to warm the house, and with Sarah's skills at canning, their pantries were full and ready to supply them with months of food. Still, concern couldn't help but nag at Conrad. Little Conrad was as healthy as could be. Yet, even with

Ron Darber under his roof, Conrad dreaded the thought of his grandson getting sick, and more so during a time of cold weather. Conrad recalled more than one winter around here that turned out pretty nasty.

And if I ever had to leave and find help, the snow would make the journey that much harder, he thought.

He then looked back down at his grandchild. Little Conrad pushed up his shoulders and made a soft cooing sound.

"Hey little guy," he said softly, "I know it's asking a lot on your second day out in the world, but I'm just hoping you can handle things okay for a while, so we can get through this winter without any trouble."

———

TOM STOOD BACK from the small wooden crib. "So, what do you think?"

Sarah and Carla surrounded him on either side. Carla pushed on the wood. "It feels steady."

"You didn't treat this with any chemicals, did you?" Sarah leaned over and sniffed the wood.

"Treat it with chemicals? No," Tom replied, "I cut it, sanded it down real good, screwed it together, and here we are."

Tom was proud of the crib he had constructed for Carla and Liam's bedroom. It wasn't very complicated, just a small bed with a wooden banister surrounding it. To him, it seemed a perfect fit for a growing baby—if his mother and grandmother approved. It had taken weeks to build the crib right, but Tom's skills quickly had improved from his initial attempts.

The great thing about wood that if it sucks, I can always throw it in the fire for warmth, Tom thought with a slight chuckle.

Carla felt along the wooden panels. "You sure there's nothing sticking out? No screws or nails?"

"No, I checked several times. I used small screws, and the few that did stick out, I just cut off the sharp edges and capped the surfaces. It should be perfectly fine," Tom replied.

"Okay." Carla smiled. "It looks great. Thanks." She reached out and hugged Tom.

Upon parting, Sarah added, "Is there any loose sawdust? You said you sanded this thing real good, right?"

"Oh, that's right." Carla leaned close to the wood and sniffed it. "Because if my baby starts sneezing, this thing's going."

Tom braced his forehead with his fingers. "Well, I guess we always can use this for the chickens if it doesn't work out."

———

STROLLING DOWN THE BACK PORCH, Conrad held his namesake in his arms as he spoke. "Now all this out here, when you learn how to run, you're going to have all the open space you want. See, when your dad was your age, kids had fast food, movies and video games, but you're going to have clean air, open fields, and a lot of hard work to make you a real physical specimen. Not to mention a lady killer."

He said all this knowing Liam was standing nearby. In fact, every time Conrad paced close to the younger Drake, he raised his voice and widened his grin. Liam tried pretending not to hear, but he couldn't hide his occasional smile at his father's sense of humor.

As for little Conrad, the baby simply looked up at his grandpa from time to time, but didn't focus much. The child's blue eyes now regularly were open, except for naptimes. In the past few weeks since his birth, little Conrad had shown all the signs of a healthy baby boy.

A few dark circles underlined Liam's eyes. Those "healthy signs" included crying for meals, and Liam had been the "lucky" one to tend them. Liam wanted to help Carla rest and regain her strength following the birth. However, it didn't help that little Conrad tended to be fussier when his dad held him. On the other hand, little Conrad responded well to his grandfather. Since Conrad stayed up late, the older man was on hand to help his son out on a few occasions. Carla said not to worry, that little Conrad would warm up to his dad soon.

Tom pushed open the door. "Well," he said, "they seem to like the crib except for everything about it."

He slapped the side of his right hip. "I'm surprised they didn't fret over the molecular composition of the wood."

"They're women. You can't fix that," Conrad said.

"If you weren't holding that baby, I'd kick your ass!" Camilla called through the open door, which hadn't fully closed behind Tom.

Conrad held up little Conrad's head. "Well, kid, looks as though I can't put you down. You're going to have to protect me."

Tom cleared his throat. "Anyway, about the crib..."

"Don't worry about it," Liam said, "It looks great. I really appreciate it. I think little Conrad will be fine."

Tom dug into his right jeans pocket. "Actually, I also was thinking of making him some toys." Then he pulled out a small piece of wood. "This is my first attempt." He waved his effort in the air, a wooden wafer cut in the shape of an animal.

"Anteater?" Liam asked.

"Horse," Tom replied.

Liam nodded. "Well, we can tell him it's an alien horse. Actually, I've been thinking about diapers. We bartered for a fresh supply not too long after we first came here, but we need a lot more. They've been a godsend to have when the cloth ones still are drying. Little Conrad is a regular poop machine."

"You haven't gone into town recently at all. I don't think since fall," Tom said.

"Actually, not since before we tussled with Kurt,"

Conrad said. "I think we are overdue to get out and replenish our supplies. The snow's been pretty light the past couple of weeks. Maybe if we take care of this now, we can get out in front of any bad storms."

————

SARAH CHASED after Liam as he walked down the hall toward the living room. "Liam, are you sure about this?"

"No. Actually, I'd rather stay by my son and my girl's side." Liam turned to his mother. "But, one of us should be there to look around for toys for little Conrad. Plus, I don't want Dad going alone. We won't be riding our bikes, so it's going to take about a full day to hike to Hooper City."

"Which is why I'd like to go along," Camilla said as she passed in front of Liam as he entered the living room.

"No, I need you to stick around here and help protect the home." Conrad was squatting near the sofa, zipping up a backpack. "Can't divide us up too much. Besides, if Liam and I have to duck off the road into the woods, I'd rather have a small party that can move in and out quickly. Too many people can be more easily spotted."

Camilla smirked as Conrad stood up. "You always got it figured out."

"Hey, always have a plan or two." Conrad took Camilla by the shoulders. "Don't worry. Hooper

City's not far and I'm sure there won't be any problems between here and there."

"Don't you find it a bit weird that Nigel's never
shown up in months?" Camilla asked.

Conrad gave it some thought. Camilla made a
good point. Why would he suddenly disappear?
Granted, Nigel checked in on them after the war with
Kurt's men, but he hadn't showed up since, or even
sent one of his men to check on them.

"Well, I guess he's been occupied," Conrad finally
said, "I'm sure there's nothing wrong, but I'll be on
guard."

———

CONRAD AND LIAM'S boots made soft crunching
sounds in the snow as the men trudged toward
Hooper City. Fortunately, the road wasn't completely
covered with snow. Thanks to the road's small high
rise, the street maintained enough of a shape in the
snow to remain recognizable.

"I do miss the bikes," Liam said.

Conrad adjusted the strap on his backpack. "Oh,
I think there's a certain charm to a nice hike down
the road." He chuckled. "Grandpa's got to take it
easy, you know."

Liam chuckled along with his dad, which led to a
soft cough. The harsh air was drying his throat,
making it a little hard to talk. "You're going to start
making that excuse from now on, about how

'grandpa' needs someone to take over more of the chores."

"Oh, don't be so suspicious. I'll only do that half the time," Conrad replied.

Liam pulled out his copy of the state map again. He never had been this far from his father's homestead since he had moved there with Carla, and despite the long hike to Redmond to find his mother months before, he still was not used to long hikes across the land without the benefit of a car with a GPS. On the other hand, his father had remained calm throughout the hours of walking, as if long hikes were in his blood.

He never stops amazing me, Liam thought. *It's going to be incredible to have little Conrad grow up like this. It's going to be nothing like when I was a kid. Growing food, milking goats, raising chickens, hiking through the woods. Hell, if the country doesn't recover, if we don't get machines working again, he may never even learn how to drive a car.*

By now they had reached a turnoff that would take them into Hooper City. Before long, the sign that said, "Welcome to Hooper City" emerged into view. The snow-covered roofs of houses and stores soon followed.

Before they could step into town, a lone male gestured to them. He was seated in a folding chair with a telescope aimed at the sky above. "Hey," the man said, "you two shouldn't be walking in the open.

Conrad took a step closer, his hand wandering down to his belt where he kept his gun. The older

Drake was always on his guard. From the looks of this man, he didn't seem dangerous. He wore a long gray beard that dangled a half a foot from his chin and camouflage clothing. The man had a rifle next to him, but it was nowhere near his fingers.

"Why is that, sir?" Conrad asked.

The man gestured above. "You never know when they might spot you."

Liam looked back up. The sky was covered with gray clouds. Nothing moved except the occasional flock of birds. "Who? The swallows?" he asked.

"No! Them! The one world army! They got metal birds up there, drones, sighters, looking to spot any human activity," the man responded.

Oh brother, Liam thought. *This guy's obviously a little off his rocker*. But part of Liam wasn't entirely sure. The drastic changes in the world had prepared him to believe a lot of things he would have dismissed prior.

"I never heard anything about a one world army. Is this a new outfit?" Conrad asked.

"Oh, it is. We got word from outside town that they're swarming all across the country." The male jabbed his thumb in the direction of town. "They'll tell you all about it. I'm the watchman."

"Well, we're just simple traders. I take it we're okay to go in?" Conrad asked.

"Sure, sure, you look okay." The man settled back into his chair. "I mean, almost all the town's trained for gun use. So, if you're looking to start trouble..."

He laughed. "Well, be prepared to meet Jehovah in the flesh!"

Conrad and Liam left the "watchman" behind and hiked into town. "Boy, that guy really is a little..." Liam aimed his finger at the side of his head and spun his digit around a few times.

"Maybe." Conrad pressed his lips together hard. "But crazy or not, he's probably heard something new that we ought to check out."

"Isn't everyone always worried about a 'one world army?'" Liam asked, "That's like the usual conspiracy stuff, along with the Illuminati and stuff like that."

"It's true stuff like that has been on people's minds for a long time, but times have changed. Enough army equipment somewhere could have been shielded from the solar burst to still be operational," Conrad said as they walked into the first stores. "The problem is, we don't know if they're friendly or not."

Liam was about to respond when a male-female couple stepped into view. The male held a pair of binoculars to his face, looking at the sky above. After a few seconds, he lowered his binoculars and nodded to the lady beside him. The two then crossed the street.

Liam turned toward his dad. Conrad flashed him a look that said, "Maybe there is something to this one world army thing."

CHAPTER SIX

NIGEL GAZED at the table of preserved fruits and vegetables. "Thank God." He picked up one of the jars and gazed at the sliced pears inside. "We cut it a little closer than I would have liked, but, at least none of us is going to starve this winter. In fact, I think we have some leeway."

On the other side of the table, Jeff Clement sighed. "I'd feel a little better if..." He chuckled. "It's hard not to worry anymore."

"Look, we've been okay so far." Nigel gazed at the small storeroom of Hooper Feed, although nowadays it largely supplied human food. Before the solar event, Nigel Crane was just a simple store owner. Now he had become a part of the town's leadership, which meant he was a sounding board for all the town's concerns.

"Maybe Hooper City is too far off the map. Let's face it, aside from Omaha and Lincoln, what is there

out here but tiny towns and a bunch of farmland?"
Nigel smiled, but the discomfort in his voice cut
down his efforts to reassure Jeff.

Before Nigel's store employee and friend could
reply, a young man strolled in through the front door.
"Mister Nigel?" The youngster wiped his thickly
bearded face.

"Ah, good!" Nigel pointed to the box behind him.
"All packed and ready to go."

The man nodded. "I'll get right to it." He leaned
over and picked it up. With his well-muscled
physique, it seemed he could pick up two boxes at
once with little strain on his body. He quickly carried
the load out the door.

"Think Lance will break another delivery record?"
Jeff asked.

"Wouldn't surprise me." Nigel laughed. "Although
rumor has it that new girl, Tracy, I think her name is,
yeah she's got an eye for that kid. He might be a little
late, if you know what I mean."

Just then, Reginald Johnson, or "Reg" as he was
popularly known, pushed open the door. "Hey. The
crowd's getting a little bigger around the memorial."

"I know, but I told you to represent me over
there. There's nothing pressing. I've got work to do
here." Nigel didn't want to add that he was tired of
fielding questions about the latest news, plus he felt
Reg was a better "people person" than he was. Town
business was just plain exhausting for Nigel lately.

"Yeah, but Conrad's shown up." Reg stood in the

doorway, the dim light shining on the middle-aged man's ebony skin. "Kyle, the same Kyle who runs our mail to the center of town, he saw him on Jasper Street."

"Conrad?" Jeff asked.

"No need to tell me which Conrad that is." Nigel marched to the door.

"Jeff, take care of the shop." As he emerged outside, he stopped suddenly, then turned to Reg. "Hey, go track down Lance and let him know about Conrad. If he needs to lay low for a bit, that's okay."

Reg nodded. "You don't think Conrad would take anything out on the kid?"

Nigel scratched his chin. "Probably not, but let's just be careful."

————

CONRAD SCRATCHED his right ear as he approached the World War II memorial. It was one of the oldest standing features of Hooper City, a small statue of an American soldier holding his rifle in the air. It wasn't fancy, about twice the height of an average adult male. Before the solar event, the memorial wasn't heavily attended. People took it for granted. Today, it was an enduring reminder of America's triumph over great adversity and perhaps, for many people, a symbol of what they could overcome in the days ahead.

Right now, about thirty people milled about the

grounds, separated into groups of three and four, chatting among each other.

Liam tapped Conrad on the shoulder. "Dad." The younger Drake pointed to a man standing apart from the crowd. He was holding binoculars to his eyes. "Check that out."

"Let me guess, he's bird watching," Conrad said, half-jokingly.

Liam shook his head. "With all these people watching the skies, I think we definitely can say there's a problem here."

"Hey!" A short man with a curly white beard walked up to the pair. "Conrad! Well I'll be. We thought you were dead."

Conrad composed himself. "I guess it's not common knowledge that I survived my run-in with Kurt's boys. You're Johnny Metz. The fella who runs a small farm on the west edge of town."

"That's me, sir." He then pointed to Liam. "This must be yours. He kinda looks like you."

"Liam." Liam reached out and offered his hand. Johnny shook it.

"So, what's the deal around here?" Conrad asked, "I'm not saying I expected regular house calls, but it's weird how everything out of Hooper City went dark."

Johnny nodded. "Well, we have been a little..." He rocked his hand back and forth. "...wary lately, if you catch my drift. We've been focusing on gun drills, protection measures, and things such as that. A lot of people don't even want to leave town if they can help it."

"Really? Why's that?" Conrad asked.

Johnny didn't get a chance to respond. "Well, long time no see!" Nigel called as he approached.

Conrad quickly excused himself and walked over to Nigel with Liam close behind. "No kidding." Conrad extended his hand. Nigel took it and gave it a shake. "I was wondering if everything was alright. I know we don't have the postal service anymore, but I'm curious why no one has stopped by in the past few months."

"I guess we've been keeping to ourselves too much lately," Nigel said.

"And watching the skies, too. You don't have a UFO problem, do you?" Liam asked.

"Well, if you mean we may have a problem with unwanted visitors from the skies, maybe." Nigel looked down the street. "Let me treat you two to a nice meal at my store, and then I'll fill you in."

————

"AT FIRST, we started hearing rumors over the ham radio," Nigel said as he walked toward the table where Conrad and Liam were seated. Nigel quickly had erected a folding table with folding chairs for Conrad and Liam to to enjoy their meal.

"Someone would see a plane in the sky, or they'd hear about a convoy of trucks going up a country road to a big city. Last month, the stories kicked into overdrive. Soldiers with different accents would show up in the cities. A whole bunch of them swarmed into Chicago. Then, they started moving south. Two weeks ago, they hit St. Louis. One wave has broken off to head for Texas. Another..." Nigel bit his lower lip.

"Well, another's headed in our general direction. I figured maybe Kansas City on the Kansas-Missouri border, but the chatter says they'll hit all fifty states in any case, even if they do it in small caravans."

"Who?" Liam asked.

"A coalition army," Jeff replied. "Military units from all across the world that still had functioning equipment pooled together. They declared them- selves a world relief organization and started fanning out across the globe. Basically, it's a one world government."

"Martial law," Nigel added, "That's basically what it is."

"They got the men and the technology. Nobody can stand up against them, even if they wanted to. The moment they show up, they're the new kings of your city," Jeff said.

"Everyone in Hooper City's heard about it," Nigel said, "As you can imagine, we're on edge here. Our town meetings are all about the latest develop- ments, since, of course, we don't get cable news anymore."

Conrad rested his chin on the top of his right

hand. "Damn. To think I didn't know anything about this."

"You couldn't have," Liam said.

"Are you kidding? I could have fired up the ham radio and checked around. I've done that before. Shit. I was so occupied with getting things ready for Carla that I didn't stop and look around at what was going on over my very head."

"Don't feel too bad. I didn't run over and give you any head's up." Nigel rested his head in his hands. "Maybe I hoped the stories would come to nothing. But now we have to prepare for the worst."

———

CONRAD CAST one more look at Liam talking with Jeff in the back room before returning his attention to Nigel. The pair gathered in Nigel's back office to discuss some business that was for Nigel's ears only.

"Jeff should be able to round up what you need for the baby." Nigel grinned. "I'll be damned. I couldn't imagine you chasing around your house after a little baby."

"He'll be crawling before I know it, I'm sure." Conrad gripped his right arm. "At least I hope so."

"Oh, come in, you're in prime shape for a man your age. How many sixty-year-olds could take on a small army and win?" Nigel asked.

"Yeah, so what will fate do but possibly dump a bigger army on my doorstep?" Conrad asked.

"You heard Jeff. They may never show up here at all," Nigel said.

"Anyway, let's get down to business. Did you gather all the supplies from my order?" Conrad asked.

Nigel nodded. "I figured one day you'd show up asking for that package." He reached into his pants pocket and pulled out a folded-up piece of paper. "I was planning on making the run over to your place once the commotion around here cooled."

"Forget about it. Just as long as it's here, that's all that matters," Conrad said.

"I slipped word to Reg to send it over here." Just then, there was a knock on the side door in the hall. "Ah! Probably it now." He rushed out to the door and opened it.

Almost immediately, he shut the door.

Conrad raised an eyebrow. "Nigel?"

The store owner turned and glanced over his shoulder. "One moment." He then quickly slipped through the door and shut it, to Conrad's puzzlement. For the next few minutes he heard a series of harsh whispers on the other side of the door. Nigel was talking to somebody, but about what, Conrad couldn't figure out.

Then the door opened halfway, enough to permit Nigel through. His face was slightly bowed, but his eyes glared up at Conrad. "Delivery's here."

"Alright. Let's see it," Conrad said.

Nigel reached behind him and opened the door as if he didn't really want to do so. He revealed a young, bearded man clutching a taped-up cardboard box. The man stepped inside until he was two steps from Conrad's chest.

"Thanks, son. I don't guess I have to sign for this," Conrad said.

The young man's eyes were locked in a tight gaze, as if the courier was studying Conrad. Even so, nothing seemed out of the ordinary. No reason presented itself to explain Nigel's behavior.

Conrad reached out and took it. "Thanks." Conrad shuffled it around in his arms. "Definitely feels like everything's here."

"Do you want to check it?" the man asked.

"No, I'll handle that later. Thanks a lot." Conrad chuckled. "So, who do I have to thank for running this over here?"

"Lance, sir," the man replied.

"Lance." Conrad nodded. "Well, thanks a million. I apologize if I can't shake your hand, but as you can see, I got mine pretty full."

"It's alright." Lance then turned to Nigel. Nigel just shot him a glare. Lance then turned and left through the door.

Conrad strolled back to the office. "Fine service, Nigel. Hey, let me open this up with the door closed."

"Fine with me." Nigel turned his gaze back to the door. "I got to take care of something myself. Nothing big. Just a little conversation with the courier."

———

NIGEL DID his best not to burst out in anger at Lance, but the sudden shock of seeing the young man at the door had set him on edge. He waited until he and Lance had trekked out to Hooper Feed's parking lot before Nigel spoke.

"What in God's name are you thinking showing up here?" Nigel asked.

"I had to see him," Lance replied quickly. "At least, I wanted to see him up close, in front of me."

"Well, thankfully, he doesn't know jack about who you really are. Now that you've satisfied your curiosity, make tracks and don't come back until I send word that he's left town," Nigel said.

"You really that afraid that he'll do something?" Lance asked.

Nigel paced around in a small circle before answering. "I figured you wanted sanctuary. Well, I'm giving it to you." Then he let out a breath that turned to mist in the cold air. "No, I don't think Conrad actually will plant your ass six feet under. He might slug you hard. You may need to be fitted for gold teeth afterward. I'm just saying it may be more trouble than it's worth."

"I know. Believe me, you don't know how grateful I am for not saying anything about me." Lance turned toward the store. "But maybe I should stop running from my problems."

"So, do you want me to tell him?" Nigel asked.

Lance waved him off. "No. No. I'll handle it if I want to do it. I won't come back again until he's gone."

Nigel nodded. "Alright. Good, good. That'll help me out a lot."

As Lance started his march down the street, Nigel pondered the young man's countenance. The courier willingly had sought out Conrad and stood before him without buckling or trembling. Indeed, this was not the same man who drove into town in a pickup truck stolen by a gang of marauders, who cowered in fear at the thought of being recognized by Kurt's men.

I never thought I'd be a community leader, Nigel thought. *I guess Lance never thought he'd be anything other than just a layabout and a wimp.*

He walked back to his store.

CHAPTER SEVEN

CONRAD FLASHED his light around the homestead. There was no movement, not so much as a squirrel running across the grass.

"Looks good so far," Liam said behind him as he flashed his light from side to side.

Conrad slowly approached the front porch. Coming home in the dark like this may not have been the wisest course of action, but the trip during the last few hours had gone off without any problems. In fact, approaching the homestead in the dark might have been wiser, as they could surprise any possible intruders.

As soon as his boots touched down on the porch, the front door suddenly flew open. Camilla emerged, shotgun in hand.

"I see I get my usual greeting," Conrad deadpanned.

Camilla, dressed in a tattered old blue robe, rolled

her eyes. "I saw the light beams outside and I freaked for a moment. I thought the men in black showed up."

"Well, I thank you kindly for not blowing our heads off," Conrad said as Liam hurried up the porch steps while dimming his light.

Camilla backed inside, permitting the two Drake men into their home. "So, I guess everything went alright?"

"Diapers, toys, we got it all," Conrad said. Then he placed his pack onto the floor by the sofa. "City was in good shape."

"Good shape except for everyone watching the skies," Liam said.

"Yeah." Conrad quickly shut and locked the door. "Cammie, we might have some trouble afoot. Liam can fill you in. I need some time to do some checking over the airwaves."

"Is this another man from your past showing up to steal your ranch?" Camilla asked.

"No." Conrad started down the hall. "Much bigger."

———

As CONRAD SAT down in front of his ham radio, he fumed silently at himself. To think that he didn't bother to turn on this little baby and see what was going on in the world. Was he so wrapped up with preparing for little Conrad's arrival, or had he turned in on himself so much that he forgot there was a world around him?

"I am one stupid son of a bitch," he muttered as crackling sounded through the speaker. He steadied the microphone up to his lips.

"Good evening," he spoke, "This is Drake, just checking to see what's going on under the stars tonight. I'm a man who's been out of the loop lately. Anyone got the latest headlines? It can be local, national, whatever you've heard."

Conrad waited and waited. Nothing. He scratched his left arm. He didn't like this. The last time he broadcast, it was no problem finding somebody to chat with. Did the silence mean something?

"Easy," Conrad said to himself, "Maybe you're broadcasting into the wrong time zone. A lot of people may still be snoozing." He almost laughed at himself.

He was on the verge of getting up for a drink of water when the speaker crackled fiercely. "Hello?" It was a male's voice, and it sounded a bit familiar.

"Hey." Conrad quickly spoke up. "This is Drake. You're coming in loud and clear."

"This is Red," the voice replied.

"Red? Hey, I remember you! We chatted several months back, not long after the solar event. How are you doing, sir?"

"Well, we're managing," Red said, "What about you?"

Conrad wondered how much he should divulge,

not only because his story might sound a little outlandish, but he was beginning to wonder if anyone could be listening in on his transmission. "Well, there's been some local trouble, but we got through it. But I do have some good news. I'm a grandfather now."

Red laughed. "Well, congratulations. That's amazing. I'm actually in the same boat as you are. My oldest son had a daughter two months ago."

"Incredible. Another hand for the farm?" Conrad chuckled.

"Yeah, I guess we're all farm hands now," Red replied, "I hate to say it, but we could use the help. My brother got bit by a snake this past September. It was pretty ugly. We had to amputate his foot. That's what happens when you can't drive to a hospital."

"At least he's still around. Sometimes you can't ask for more than that," Conrad said.

"True that. So, what can I do for you?" Red asked.

"I'm a man in need. Word on the grapevine is that a new army has come together and is occupying the big cities. Do you know anything about that, or is it just wild talk?"

"No wild talk. A small force has occupied Pierre. That's our state capital. But from what my friend told me, that was nothing compared to the party set up in Chicago. We're so far off the grid that nobody's come around here, but they're definitely hitting the countryside. They move into the small towns in small bands. Many of the soldiers then start relocating people."

"Wait. Hold up. Relocating?" Conrad cut in.

"Yeah. It's a way of pooling everyone together. They say they can't spread themselves out enough to provide for all the people they meet, so they do it this way to maximize resources."

"Relocation," Conrad muttered, "Do the people go willingly?"

"I don't know. The army offers food and medicine, so I imagine no one wants to turn that down. But here's the really scummy thing about it. The aid they're delivering is coming from other people under their protection. They determine who has a surplus, take the excess, and distribute it to areas in need."

Conrad's skin suddenly grew cold. A military with a self-declared right to take from others was one of the worst scenarios he could imagine.

"And on whose authority do they do that?" Conrad asked, "Who's giving the orders?"

"Got me. I never got a name on who's running the army. My friend passed along a story of an official with a Scottish accent, of all things. I asked him if he was wearing a kilt," Red said.

Conrad laughed. "Should have asked him if he painted his face and had long hair."

"William Wallace?" Red asked.

"Yep. Guess you've seen *Braveheart*, too."

"Wore out my old VHS copy. But yeah, I got nothing on who's leading them, but it sounded like it's more like a U.N. thing, people with different accents, wearing different flags on their shirts."

"That sounds more like an invasion to me," Conrad said.

"Yeah. I feel that way, too."

Conrad chatted some more with Red, but he received little more information. Still, between the news of relocation and the seizing of resources, it was enough to set him on edge. No wonder the folks in Hooper City were so nervous.

His thoughts were interrupted when a jolt of pain struck his right arm. "Damn." He had turned his arm only to receive a quick burst of agony. His arm had been bothering him for a while, but it was getting worse.

He had to talk to Ron Darber as soon as possible.

———

As usual, Conrad rose before everyone else did. He waited in the front room for everyone else to rouse from their sleep. He knew they'd be coming to see him before they started their daily chores. They all wanted to hear how the trip to Hooper City went. Conrad knew they'd be in for much more disturbing news.

Conrad waited until everyone had emerged into the living room. Carla was among the last, cradling little Conrad. The older Conrad smiled at the sight of him. The newborn could lift anybody's spirits.

Conrad and Liam got started talking about their journey into town. However, Conrad then had to add what he learned about the military, specifically their relocation and supply redistribution efforts.

Camilla reacted with intense interest, cutting in to ask questions, while Ron Darber, Sarah, and Tom listened carefully. Carla's attention was wrapped up with little Conrad, especially when the little one awoke and cried for food. Carla excused herself into the kitchen to breastfeed her son, but remained within earshot.

"Well, what a shock." Camilla rose from her seat and walked over to Conrad. "Sooner or later the next world order was going to come along. Guess they saw the carnage and decided to take advantage."

"So, that's it?" Sarah asked, sounding a lot more skeptical than Camilla. "I mean, it sounds as if you just heard a bunch of rumors. Has anybody around here actually seen these soldiers?"

"No," Conrad said, "I asked, but nobody in Hooper City encountered a single one of them, and I didn't hear any first-hand accounts on the airwaves last night."

"It could be our army getting back on its feet," Tom said. "I mean, why would we think everything in the country would be knocked flat on its back? I'm sure the government prepares for things like this. They probably had trucks and supplies stashed away in case of catastrophes, and only now they're getting up to speed."

"Whoever it is, it sounds as though they're throwing their weight around. I'm all for giving aid to people, but ripping it out of people's hands at the point of a gun is another matter altogether," Conrad said.

"Well, I say we get ready in case they decide to show up," Camilla said.

"Wait, are they coming?" Tom asked.

"Nigel said they're headed in this general direction, but you got to figure they'll find us sooner or later." Conrad stood up from his chair. "So, that means we have to make plans. The trees I stuck in the driveway can stop ordinary civilian trucks, but an overwhelming force of men can still get around them."

Sarah leaned forward in her seat. "You're making plans to fight them?"

"Of course. Worse comes to worse, we have to be ready if they show up looking to take the farm," Conrad said matter-of-factly.

"Conrad." Sarah shook her head. "Don't you think that's going overboard a little? We still don't know these people are bad."

"If they're throwing people off their land, that's bad enough for me," Conrad said.

"No kidding," Camilla said.

————

THE MEETING WRAPPED UP, with everyone breaking

off to handle their chores. However, while the living room cleared out, Conrad quickly caught Darber by the arm before he could depart the room.

"Hey, Ron," he said, urgently, but as quietly as he could so to not get the attention of anyone who might be within earshot. "We need to chat."

"Yes, we do," Darber said, calmly, as if he had expected Conrad to approach him like this. "I finished all the tests."

Conrad released his friend. "Then we have to talk in private, now."

———

CONRAD CLOSED his bedroom door as silently as he could once Darber had slipped inside. He then took the extra step of checking his window. It was cranked shut. If they kept their voices fairly low, they shouldn't carry. Almost everyone but Carla was outside anyway, so their conversation should be private.

Darber sat down, stone-faced. He had been used to giving news like this. Conrad was certain of that. The rancher vowed to take whatever Darber threw at him, even if it was the worst news he could receive.

Darber didn't mince words. "It's malignant. It's attached to your right tricep muscle, just above your elbow."

Conrad sucked in his lip a little. "How much time do I have?"

"Without treating it, probably less than six months, depending on when it spreads. Unfortunately, without functioning CT scans to work with, I can't tell if it has spread anywhere else. But, assuming that it is localized in your arm, we still can operate on it."

"You can do surgery, even without electrical equipment?" Conrad asked.

"Yes. It's not very complicated, and with the supplies you brought back, I think we'll be in fine shape." Darber looked at the box on Conrad's dresser. "Of course, you'll still have a recovery period, and your arm will be weak for a while. You'll have to be cautious or you could fracture the bone."

Conrad turned to the box. Since Darber had shared his first inklings about Conrad's possible condition, he had made sure to ask Nigel if he could procure certain medical instruments. Nigel had indeed come through, and not a moment too soon.

"But I'll still be able to do my jobs around here," Conrad said.

"There will be some diminishment, I imagine. With exercise, you could re-strengthen your arm, but you'll have to be cautious going forward. It would be easier on you if you were a young man. At your age, even being in as good a condition as you are, recovery will take longer."

"Can you give me the odds?" Conrad asked.

"No guarantees. I'm sorry. That's the best I can do. But even if we're successful in removing the tumor, you'll have to keep a close watch on this for the rest of your life. Cancer reoccurring always is a possibility, and given how much of our medical technology we've lost, we easily could not see it coming."

Conrad nodded. "Thanks, Ron."

"Are you planning to let the others know?" Darber asked.

"Not yet," Conrad said quickly, "This is one thing I don't want to drop on their heads if I can help it. I'll give it some thought."

"When do you want to operate?" Darber asked.

"Like I said, I'll give it some thought," Conrad said.

CHAPTER EIGHT

SARAH FOLLOWED Tom into their bedroom. Tom stripped off his shirt, then tossed the sweaty garment into the laundry basket near the foot of the bed. The pair exchanged some small talk, but Tom never once addressed the burning question on Sarah's mind.

Finally, she couldn't take it. "So, what do you think?" she asked.

"About what?" Tom asked.

"C'mon, Tom, you know what I mean. I haven't heard one peep out of you about this whole military situation."

Tom turned to her. "I don't know. Sounds like it could be bad news."

"But what if it isn't?" Sarah slowly approached him. "C'mon, you know how crazy talk can spread. What if these soldiers have a good reason for shifting supplies around? Some people obviously need help more than others. God knows we're in pretty good shape. I only can imagine what it's like if you're living in a town like Redmond, starving to death in the streets."

Tom only could speak an "I know" before Sarah continued. When she wanted to, Sarah could speechify for over an hour.

"No one has said these soldiers are mowing people down with guns. No one has talked about..." She shivered. "...abusing women. I just think there could be a good explanation for all of this. And besides, you know the American military has contingency plans for this kind of stuff. They plan for nuclear war. They plan for natural disasters. This isn't that different. They must have had vehicles and planes tucked away for emergencies. Maybe it took this long to gather everyone together for the rescue operation."

"Look, I get it," Tom said, quickly, "Old Red, White and Blue's coming to save us. I'd love to believe that. But you know militaries also can be bad news. We don't know who's leading it. It could be the president, but it also could be some general or nutcase terrorist."

"I know. I'm not saying just jump in and hug them. But Conrad sounds like he's going to fight them without even checking to see if they're on our side." Sarah cringed.

"I mean, God, we now have a little baby. You want to see little Conrad have to dodge bullets before he can even walk? It was one thing when the party was all us, but it's not." She pushed her gray hair away from her cheeks and forehead. "Tom, I want my little grandson to be safe. I want Liam and Carla to grow old. I want the fighting to end. Is it so hard to believe our lives can be normal again?"

Tom shook his head. "I do, too." He sat down on the bed. "With all the desperate people and nutjobs out there, a booming farm like this always is going to be a target. But if the military is with us, they could protect us."

"That's right!" Sarah smiled as she sat down next to him. "We finally could have peace. I don't care if I have to work a little harder to provide for someone else. Let me do it if I never have to pick up a gun and patrol this house ever again. Let soldiers do that."

"But you know Conrad's going to hate the idea. He won't trust them, not one bit," Tom said.

"I know. He might chew my arm off for even suggesting it, but it's his grandchild, too. This is his family. He can't see anything in life beyond his warrior persona. He's always been like that."

"Let me guess. He told you about his favorite Western?" Tom asked.

"*Shane*?" Sarah asked.

"No, *The Searchers*," Tom replied, "But *Shane*'s a close second."

Sarah frowned. "I never knew that. Never mind. You know what I'm getting at."

"Don't worry." Tom wrapped his arm around her.

"I'll talk to him about it. I'll take the arrows for both of us."

———

CONRAD SWITCHED on the ham radio. He unfolded the piece of paper, then tuned the radio to the frequency written on it.

"Tigerbait, this is Drake," Conrad said.

"Read you loud and clear," Nigel's voice filtered through the speakers.

"Hey. It's not a telephone, but it'll do," Conrad said, "So, where the hell did you get 'Tigerbait' as a call sign?"

"I've fished since I was seven years old," Nigel replied, "I've got quite a story behind that."

"Tell me later. Have you heard anything new out there about our new friends? I've got some disquieting news on my end."

"Lay it on me," Nigel said, sounding tired, "I don't have anything new to share."

Conrad told Nigel the story of the army taking supplies and redistributing them to other areas. Nigel didn't sound shocked at all. "Sounds like what I thought," he said with a sigh. "Conrad, if this comes our way, there's nothing we can do about it. We're toast. Most of our men are armed, but we just can't compete with trucks and machine guns. We just have to hope they're benevolent."

Conrad refrained from saying what was really on

his mind and pushed forward with the issue he really had called about. "I hope you don't mind, but I do have a favor to ask. You know that package you delivered to me the other day? I'm about ready to use a lot of it, and I'd like to ask for your help."

"This is about you, isn't it?" Nigel asked.

Conrad huffed loudly. "Yeah."

"Is it bad?" Nigel asked.

"It's not good, but there's a chance I'll pull through this. I'm going to give it my all. Will you give me a hand?"

"Sure," Nigel said, "Just tell me what you need."

———

CONRAD RUBBED HIS EYES. Once again, he was up before the sun rose. His body instinctively knew when to rise, though in the past few weeks climbing out of bed had become a chore. It was as if his discussions with Darber had alerted his body that he was sick and told him to act that way. He massaged his right arm quickly to try soothing the latest ache.

He wished Darber's diagnosis was the only thing he had to worry about. Nigel's story plus Red's account only had thrown another wrench in the works. Ironically, learning about the new army had helped him focus. Conrad knew he couldn't let his health issues slide. He had to deal with the tumor to stay alive, to guard his home and family.

If Ron had told me this just a year ago, I wouldn't have

cared much about it. What did I have to live for then? Dying of cancer would have taken me out peacefully.

He was closing in on a big decision. However, that still left the shadow of this new military to deal with.

Conrad poked his head out of the doorway into the living room. A figure shifted in the easy chair by the couch. Conrad's pulse quickened. Nobody was up this early in this house but him.

An adult male's head turned. Tom blinked his bloodshot eyes. The man looked as if he hadn't slept at all last night.

"Tom." Conrad approached. "You look like you've been run over by a semi."

Tom closed his eyes and tried to laugh, but it came out as a cough. "I think I'd prefer a semi."

"Let me grab you some coffee." Conrad turned to the kitchen. "It's too early for a drink. I can't have you drunk while you're cutting the wood." He chuckled.

A few minutes later, Conrad came back with a steaming mug of coffee. Tom took it and drank deeply. "Thanks," Tom said afterward. Conrad brought his own cup, which he sipped as he sat in the chair opposite Tom.

"You alright? I hope you're not in the doghouse with Sarah," Conrad said.

"No." Tom yawned. "I've just had too much on my mind." He drank again before continuing. "We've been wondering about that army you told us about. Sounds like they could be trouble, right?"

"The whole thing just makes me itch." Conrad stared at his cup. "I don't expect the government to swoop in and say everything's peachy again, but when you've got an overwhelming military force sitting on your front lawn, that just flashes a big red light. It's even worse when they're taking what they please."

"Yeah. I figured you wouldn't trust them." Tom cleared his throat. "But maybe we should consider that they really are out here to help us. Just hear me out. We've never heard of them actually mistreating anyone, right? I mean, barbed wire, camps, executions, things like that. How about we call off the war and try getting more information?"

"Call off the war, huh?" Conrad narrowed his eyes. "Is Sarah telling you shit like that?"

"The two of us discussed it." Tom raised his finger while deepening his voice. "You know what I mean."

"I'm not saying I'd shoot them at first sight," Conrad said with some irritation, "but if they say they want my land, I am going to show them the door. I'll make sure they either leave peacefully or on a stretcher, but they will be going one way or the other."

"But that's just it. What if there's someplace better for us to go?" Tom asked,

"You can stow that talk right there. We're not resettling anywhere," Conrad cut in.

"I didn't say we were," Tom quickly replied. "I just said it might be worth hearing out."

"And where would we go? Where out there is

going to be safe for us? The best place we could be is off the road in a house like this. They'll probably offer up a refugee camp where you live night and day at the hand of whatever warden's running the place. Forget it."

"Maybe they've retaken a small town or a city," Tom suggested.

"Same old situation. God help us, you don't want to be inside an urban area with a bunch of soldiers looking over your shoulder. Something goes wrong, it's either a powder keg where you get caught by a dozen maniacs trying to kill you, or it becomes a prison where you have no rights."

Tom rubbed the tired skin around his eyes. "You really don't trust anyone, do you?"

"I trust people. Institutions, well, all the ones I like are pretty much gone now." Conrad took a long drink from his mug before placing it on the nearby end table. "But it's a fool's errand to trust an army that doesn't have any accountability. If something goes wrong, who's going to court martial them? Where's the Congress to hold hearings? Now, don't get me wrong. I didn't trust those jokers when the lights still were on. But today, we don't have those other jokers to provide any kind of check."

"So, you're not going to give this a chance?" Tom said.

Conrad scooped up his mug. "There's not a chance in Hell that I'm going to give this place up. Not now. Not after all the years I put into it." Then he walked slowly past the end table toward the space near the doorway to the kitchen. "If they come for me, if they tell me I have to go, I'd sooner burn this place down and take as many of them with me."

———

LANCE PLACED the package on Nigel's office table with a huff. "Here's the last of it."

Nigel nodded. "Thanks." The store owner rose from his seat. "Well, I guess there's no use putting it off. Lord knows a lot of people don't want me away from town in case..." He threw up his hands. "...the invaders show up. Guess I can't blame them for being scared."

"They're always talking about it, no matter where I go," Lance said.

Nigel straightened out his gray shirt. "Well, one perk of walking down State Road 22 is nobody's going to be in my ear for much of the day."

"So, no one's going with you?" Lance asked.

"It'll be a little quicker this way." Nigel started toward the open doorway. "If I run into trouble, it's just my own ass I have to worry about."

"I want to go with you," Lance said quickly, before Nigel could fully exit the room.

Nigel stopped, then turned around with a frown on his face. "Excuse me?"

Lance straightened up. "You probably shouldn't

go alone," he said, as if offering an excuse to cover what he really wanted to do.

Nigel looked at Lance as if the young man had gone mad. "You do realize I'm going to Conrad's house. The one place on Earth you want to desperately stay away from?"

"Yeah." Lance nodded. "I know. But I want to see it. I want to see his family. I want to know that nothing I did caused any..." He huffed.

"They're all alive, if that's what you mean, and no one's been crippled or suffered any lasting injuries. So, I don't think you need to worry."

Lance fidgeted. "I know, but I have to go. I need to do this. I want to see the house again, to see it all for myself."

Nigel shook his head. "You really got to soothe your conscience, don't you? What if somebody recognizes you? I'm sure somebody caught sight of you through the windows as they were trying to blow your ass away." Then Nigel pointed to Lance's face. "Of course, the new beard probably will help."

"I'll take that chance," Lance said. "Please, let me do this. If you want me to go with you and just camp out in the woods, I'll do that if it makes it easier."

Nigel quickly paced in a small circle. This was one hell of a wrinkle in his plans. By all rights, he ought to shut Lance down and head out. But would Lance decide to trail him anyway?

"Alright." Then he shot a slight glare at Lance. "But just be careful, and don't let anything slip about your involvement with Derrick." He poked Lance in the upper shoulder, though not hard. "Remember, you're walking into this. You're going to own whatever happens to you."

Lance nodded. "Yeah. I know."

CHAPTER NINE

TOM SLAPPED the piece of wood on top of the two wooden horses. "It went down like a lead balloon," Tom said.

Sarah leaned against the side of the house. "At least you survived to tell the tale," she said.

Tom took hold of the ruler on a nearby table and placed it on the board. With a pencil, he drew a guideline across it. "I tell you, you two must have had some interesting dinner conversations when you were married," he said.

Sarah crossed her arms. "Oh, believe me, I've got some stories."

Tom traced another line with his pencil on the opposite end of the lumber. "From what he said, it doesn't sound like he's going to challenge them head on, but I'm sure he's plotting a bigger defense. It wouldn't surprise me if he builds a stone wall around the house and mines every piece of dirt out to the roadside."

Sarah sighed. "This is going to be a disaster. I know Conrad's gotten us through some bad times with Derrick and Kurt, but a whole army? I'd say that's crazy even for him, but..." She threw up her arms. "The man almost never buys that things can be good. That maybe the world for once isn't out to get him. He's going to do something that's really stupid and it's going to come back and bite him hard."

Tom turned and looked Sarah full in the face. "So, what do you want to do? Are you thinking of leaving?"

Sarah folded her arms. "I'd have to leave Liam. He's not leaving his father, and, of course, Carla's not leaving him." She bowed her head.

"After all the time he lost, I suspect he'll stay with him until his dying day. And, I really can't ask him to go. It's because of me that he lost out with Conrad." She curled her fingers. "I can't leave him either. My baby, my little grandson..." She shook her head.

Tom nodded. "Then I guess we stick it out for now."

Sarah nodded back. "For now."

Tom lightly touched Sarah's bare arm. "Actually, all this doomsday talk from your ex has got me thinking about some things. If we truly have only a little time left before things go to hell again, maybe we should consider...well, you know."

Sarah's eyes widened. "Are you talking about..."

Tom smiled. "Maybe."

Sarah suddenly grabbed and hugged Tom. "Oh please, I've been hoping for this."

Tom chuckled. "Well, I'm not popping the question yet."

"Oh, I know. But this is good enough." Sarah gripped Tom a little tighter.

———

CONRAD HELD his grandson under the apple tree. "Yeah, I figured it was time you met your great grandpappy." He smiled at little Conrad, who just turned his head from side to side. The baby was bundled up well and seemed comfortable in the crisp winter air. Liam and Carla stood close by. Sarah was nowhere in sight, and neither was Tom. Conrad wasn't surprised. Sarah didn't like coming here the first time Conrad showed everyone the grave marker of his father.

Conrad turned to the stone resting in the shadow of the tree. A soft layer of snow coated the top, but much of the stone was exposed, more than enough to show off the name "James Bradford Drake" carved into it. "See, Daddy? This is your great-grandson. Sure you'd be proud as hell of him."

Conrad imagined his father in the space where the stone was. Memories of his father zipped by him, from the dark-haired surly young man Conrad knew as a kid, to the graying, frustrated middle-aged man Conrad knew as a young adult, and finally, the degraded, stroke-impaired elderly man Conrad nursed in his final days. James Drake was a man that terrified Conrad so often. And yet, coming up here and reminiscing had become slightly harder for him each time. As mixed as Conrad's feelings were, he still wished the old man was here.

Sadly, James died a year before Liam and Carla arrived at the homestead. Conrad wished he could have seen his own father's eyes when the elder Drake saw his great-grandson. Conrad wanted his father to know the family had continued and thrived. It would give the old man some comfort, knowing that despite the failures he had suffered in life, his progeny would continue and thrive.

"You know our last name, Drake, it's English for 'dragon.'" Conrad chuckled.

"That's right. The dragon. The mighty beast of legend." He looked back at the stone. "I guess we fit the name, don't we Daddy? We're both big, fierce, fire-breathing monsters."

He glanced at Liam and Carla. The pair smiled, but a bit awkwardly, as if he they didn't know how to react. Conrad decided to change the subject a little, to lighten things up. He told little Conrad, "In fact, your great-great-grandfather, my daddy's daddy, he married an Irish lady. Liam, your daddy, his first name is actually from his great-great-uncle. So, Liam's an Irish dragon." He chuckled.

Liam looked at Carla. "I guess that's why I always

loved Lucky Charms," he said. Carla playfully swatted Liam in the chest.

Little Conrad let out a small cry. "Uh oh." Conrad turned to Carla. "Either he's hungry or getting a little pooped out."

Carla reached out. "I'll take him." Conrad handed the baby over to her. "Oh, I know that sound. He is tired. C'mon sweetie, I'll put you down."

Carla started off for the homestead. Liam was about to join her, but he hung back with his father. "Are you okay, Dad?"

Conrad smiled, putting on a relaxed face. "Sure. I suppose it's just hard to think about Daddy. I wish he could have made it to see your son. Say, can I just have a moment here?"

"Sure." Liam backed up. "I'll make sure little Conrad gets tucked in."

Conrad watched his son leave. Then, he turned back to the stone under the tree, and his expression darkened.

"Yeah, I wish you were here to see the little guy. You could have seen Liam and Carla. You'd have seen how a family can be, not like the hellhole I grew up in." He pushed his lips together hard. "In the months that Carla's been here, I never once saw her cry or scream or despair the way Mama did. But you probably wouldn't have made the connection, would you? You were always too set in your ways."

He gazed at the stone. Naturally, it never would respond to him.

"Still, I wish I could talk to you. Remember when you told me Nature is the great equalizer? Well, my number might be coming up." He flexed his right fingers.

"I'd probably be with you and Mama and all the boys soon enough, but I'm not ready. If I must leave this world, then I've got to secure the future for Liam and Carla and my grandkid. Hell, for all the grandkids they'll give me, even the ones I'll never see." He bowed his head. "And right now, I don't know how the hell to do that."

It was a minute before he could look back at the grave marker. A bit of peace came over him.

"I still got time, don't I?" Conrad asked. "Well, I'll make the most of it. I'm sure there's one thing we can agree on. Liam and little Conrad are the best of the Drake men in the past four generations."

He looked at the grave one final time, and seemed to perceive a note of agreement coming from the snow-covered ground.

———

"I DON'T KNOW," Liam said as Carla folded the blanket neatly over little Conrad's feet. "He acted like something was bugging him."

"Doesn't he always act that way?" Carla asked as she made a face at little Conrad.

"No, actually, leading up to little Conrad's birth,

he was fine. I'd say he was even pretty relaxed about everything."

Carla turned to Liam. "Well, I guess visiting your own dad's grave isn't the happiest thing you can do in life, is it?"

"Guess not." Liam grimaced. "I'd hate to think of having to do that myself someday."

"Well, we did learn the origin of the Drake family name." Carla smiled. "So, our little Conrad is a dragon."

Liam laughed. "Sometimes he sounds like one, especially when he's hungry or wants you to hold him."

Carla laughed. "Yeah." Then she glanced at her child, and her expression cooled. "You know, for a moment I didn't know if Drake would be his last name. I mean, considering we're not married, I guess he could have taken my last name and been an Emmet."

Liam drew in a long breath. "I can't believe I didn't think of that."

"What, you never thought about marrying me?"

"No, no." Liam's skin burned. "I mean, in the run-up to little Conrad being born. I haven't been able to think about anything else but working the farm and getting ready for his birth." He looked into Carla's eyes and instantly felt guilty. "Maybe I thought you were my wife anyway. Actually, it's hard to think of you as anything else."

"That's sweet." Carla's smile looked a little pained

as she said it, though. "But I guess it would have been nice to have made it official. I went through a few sets of parents before I settled on the right one. Having an actual husband would make this whole family thing a little more real for me, like there's no chance it could just blow away."

Yeah. But my parents were married and that didn't stop them from splitting up. But Liam didn't dare voice that sentiment. Instead, he just looked away. Carla was right. He realized he had taken his arrangement with Carla for granted for too long. The two of them loved each other. Liam didn't doubt that. So, why not go that extra mile and make that commitment, with no caveats?

"Don't worry about it." Carla reached down and readjusted little Conrad's blanket. "I guess we've all got our hands full dealing with this crazy new world."

"Yeah," Liam said. But as he watched Carla work with their son, he vowed he would take care of this oversight, and soon.

———

DARBER HELD up the small glass vial. "My compliments to Nigel. This amount of regional anesthesia is perfect to numb your arm long enough for the operation." Then he turned to Conrad. "With this, you won't be screaming for me to put a bullet in your head to end the agony."

"I once dug a nail out of my foot. It can't be that

much worse," Conrad said, seated on the edge of his bed.

Darber shook his head. "Just thank God you won't have to find out." He put the vial in the box Conrad had brought back from Hooper City. Then he fished out a plastic bag with what appeared to be black string coiled up inside. "Before, I would have been able to use laser surgery to seal up your skin. But, fortunately, Nigel was able to find us some thread."

"Now, did he order more than what you need?" Conrad pointed to the box. "I didn't just want enough for me. Anybody living here might need i someday. Liam or Sarah or Carla could fall, maybe split open their leg or an arm."

"The incision won't be large, so I think there will be plenty left over," Darber said.

"So, I guess we're set," Conrad said.

"I'd say so. Do you still plan to keep a full lid on this?" Darber asked.

"It'd probably be for the best. If I beat this thing, I'll spare everyone the worrying. Why get them all worked up if I end up alright?"

Darber strolled in front of the window. Fresh snow fell outside. "True. But, you will be slowed down for a while and your family and friends will notice." He turned and looked right at Conrad. "Perhaps this will be the turning point."

Conrad stiffened up. "Ron, my mind's made up. The plan's set. There's nothing else to be done."

Darber nodded. He paced back to the window, where he gazed at the falling snow. "I just was thinking of Tara a few days ago. It's been so long since I last saw her. I was wondering if she's alright."

"Think she'd go by your house in Davies?" Conrad asked.

"God knows if the house is there any more. I wonder if the place burned to the ground in a riot when Kurt didn't come back. Or, perhaps the town is as quiet as a mouse." Darber ran a hand through his thinning hair. "It's been so long. I just wonder if I took her for granted. With all the chaos in this world, perhaps I should have paid more attention to her."

"Look, if you want me to help search for her, maybe put out a word on the radio, I'll do it. It's the least I can do after all you've done for me."

"I'd appreciate that. I suppose I'm just saying I wish I had someone to confide in." He sighed. "That's not something you have to worry about."

Swallowing hard, Conrad turned away. Darber had touched that nerve again. He turned his attention to the window, to the stars outside.

"Ron, I'm not sure if I can do anything but keep my cards close to the vest. I feel like I can control the world that way, at least my world." Then he grasped his right arm. "But with this damn tumor in my system, I'm just bullshitting myself, aren't I? Someday my time's going to run out."

"It'll run out for all of us sooner or later. Nobody lives forever."

"Every man will die." Conrad stood up out of bed. "But not every man will really live."

"*Braveheart?*" Darber asked.

"It's nice to know everyone I know has good taste in films," Conrad said with a smile. He had paraphrased the line from the film's main character, William Wallace. "Though it's a shame you don't like Westerns."

"I was always more into classic musicals," Darber replied as he turned once again to the window. Then he laughed.

Conrad scratched his chin. "I can't tell Liam yet. He's got too much to worry about right now with his baby. I have no right to make this his problem." He looked back to Darber. "All right, Ron, here's what we're going to do."

CHAPTER TEN

TOM WITHDREW the saw from the wood. "Damn!" That was the third time the blade had caught inside the wood. He simply couldn't concentrate as much as he wanted. Sarah's worries over Conrad's plans for the mysterious army had distracted Tom more than he wished.

Since his mind was too rattled, he stopped to ponder his own feelings about the matter. He didn't feel Conrad was a bad man, not at all. On the contrary, his time with Conrad in the city of Redmond had changed Tom considerably. The experience of fighting off Maggiano's men and freeing Sarah had shorn him of a lot of selfish and shallow thinking. In fact, Tom felt he owed Conrad for changing him.

But that didn't mean Tom would follow Conrad blindly. Conrad could be brave and resourceful, but he still was a little too eccentric and paranoid for

Tom's tastes. He didn't even feel he could call himself Conrad's friend, at least not a close one. It seemed like a floating mist accompanied Conrad wherever he went. Tom never would see a clear view of the man.

He didn't have time to think it over any longer, as two adult males approached the property from the state road. Leaving his project behind, he raced to the edge of the fence, dreading a repeat of the time he spotted Kurt's three men coming to look for Doctor Darber.

The two men carried backpacks, which wasn't odd. Without cars to drive, walks down the road could take hours or days, so travelers needed a good supply of water and food. But that backpack also could be hiding weapons.

He was about to head back to the house, to call Conrad and the others and let them know two strangers were approaching, but then Conrad himself emerged from the house, walking up to the man before he reached the driveway to the homestead. The pair chatted, but Tom was too far away to hear them.

He knows them, Tom thought. His anxiety cooled off. He realized he probably understood Conrad's mode of thinking more than he might have known, if he had to immediately suspect trouble whenever he spotted a stranger approaching.

"Damn," he said to himself.

———

CAMILLA WAS SCRUBBING some grease off the kitchen countertop when Conrad's heavy footsteps from the open doorway turned her head. She stuck her head out the door. He was approaching the hall that ran past the kitchen, with Nigel and a young bearded man beside him. Both newcomers wore backpacks, having not discarded them since they entered the home.

"Hey." Conrad said. "I invited Nigel over to help with some important housework. He brought in some muscle to give us a hand." Conrad slapped the young man on the shoulder.

The youngster reacted with a bit of undisguised horror, his eyes widening and his body flinching, but he quickly recovered.

"Oh, don't sweat it, kid. I'm just playing with you," Conrad said before turning back to Camilla. "Yeah, this is Lance. He's one of Nigel's delivery men."

"Hi." Camilla smiled at him.

Lance nodded. "Hi," he said.

Then Conrad stopped very close to Camilla. "Yeah, we're going to be indisposed for much of the day. I hope that's okay."

Camilla smiled. "Hey, whatever you want to do is fine by me."

Conrad grasped Camilla's hand and slid something into it. He smiled and walked off with Nigel and Lance.

Confused, Camilla opened her hand. Conrad had

deposited a small folded up note in it. She opened it up and silently read the contents.

Come to my room at 1 o'clock. Don't tell anyone. Conrad.

"Hey," spoke Tom from behind Camilla.

Camilla quickly folded her fingers, crumpling the paper in her hand. Then she turned around. Tom was looking down the hall. "Conrad come in here? I saw him talking with somebody outside."

"That was Nigel. He's a storeowner from Hooper City," Camilla replied.

"Oh." Tom scratched behind his head. "Well, that's one load off my mind. I wasn't sure if he was a friendly when he showed up. Is he going to be around for a while?"

"I don't know. Conrad said not to worry," Camilla replied.

Tom excused himself back outside, leaving Camilla to ponder what Conrad could be up to. She also got a weird feeling about that Lance kid. He seemed a tad nervous. Also, he was looking around at the walls, particularly at the places that had bullet holes.

No matter, she thought. *If I saw a house with a bunch of bullet holes, I'd wonder what kind of parties they were throwing.*

———

AN HOUR LATER, Camilla knocked on the bedroom door. One o'clock had just arrived. "Conrad?"

"You alone?" Conrad called through the wood.

"Yeah. Why?" Camilla answered.

"You can come in. You'll see," Conrad replied.

Camilla turned the knob and pushed the door in. As soon as she stepped through the door, Nigel took her, ushered her through, and then quickly shut the door behind her.

Conrad lay in the bed, bare chested, his arm outstretched. Darber stood there wearing gloves and a cloth mask over his face. Lance also stood in a corner of the room, his eyes darting from the box of medical supplies on the dresser to Conrad himself.

"What is all this?" Camilla asked.

"Oh, nothing too fancy, Cammie, just a little routine surgery," Conrad said.

Camilla's mouth dropped open. "Surgery?"

"I know. Surprise!" Conrad chuckled once, but quickly calmed down and grew serious when it became clear Camilla was in no mood for humor.

"I have a confession to make. I brought Ron here for more than just Carla and my grandbaby. I've had odd feelings up and down my right arm for months now. It's more than just old age aches. Doctor Ron checked me out, ran tests, did all that stuff. He confirmed it. There's a tumor in my right arm."

Camilla's eyes widened with panic. "Conrad! Good God!" She shook her head. "Is it—"

"Will it kill me? Hell yes, it could. But the doctor here thinks there could be a chance I make it out of this alright. I had hoped it was nothing, but I guess it's not the first time I've been wrong."

"How long have you known about this?" Camilla asked.

"Just suspicions until I called in Doctor Ron. I wasn't going to say anything until we had a plan in place. Now we have the supplies, we have the doctor, and we have the help. So, now it's time for me to fight this thing."

Camilla breathed heavily. "Conrad...my God. Of all the things for you to spring on me! But still, why now?"

Conrad sighed. "I know I probably don't understand this whole life partner bit. To quote my son's generation, I kinda suck at it. But I want to try making that right. Can you keep this between us?"

Camilla folded her arms. "Alright."

Conrad smiled. "Thank you, baby."

"So, what do you want me to do?" Camilla asked.

"The surgery team always could use another hand. But personally, I'd just rather have you in here while they do it. It'll help me get through it."

Camilla nodded. "Sure." She then smiled weakly.

Darber cleared his throat. "Conrad, I think we should get started."

———

A FEW HOURS LATER, Darber finished wrapping up Conrad's right arm. "Conrad, you were a model patient." Then he laughed. "Of course, the anesthesia helped."

Conrad was sitting up in the bed, groggy, his flesh covered with sweat. Camilla sat beside him. "So, what's going to happen now?" Camilla asked.

"I'll keep checking up on him as the days go by, but basically I had to remove a slight bit of muscle along with the tumor. With time, Conrad can regain most of the use of his arm, but he'll have to go easy."

"Don't worry about me," Conrad said in a slurred voice. "Easy as pie."

"Oh please. Tomorrow you'll be back out chopping wood as if nothing happened," Camilla said with a chuckle.

"I hope that is a joke," Darber said, frowning. "Conrad can recover, but not if he exerts himself."

"Ron..." Conrad coughed. "Look, I got to prepare this house. The military. Out there. Probably shouldn't have gone under the knife. But I'm...no good...to us dead."

"I'm sure you've bought yourself some time, but remember, tumors can reoccur. This doesn't mean you'll live to the ripe old age of ninety. We have to keep tabs on your health constantly until the day you die."

Nigel coughed. "Can we clean up? This room reeks."

Beside him, Lance waved a hand in front of his face. "Yeah, it smells like a flock of raccoons farted."

Conrad broke out in laughter, followed by a

sudden yelp of pain. "Ah! Damn. Nigel, your boy has a great sense of humor, but maybe you two should let me be for a while. Go enjoy the hospitality of my home."

As Darber reached for the window and opened it, Camilla asked, "But what do we tell everyone?"

"Tell them I'm just under the weather," Conrad whispered, "I'm sixty. They won't ask too many questions."

"But you will tell them eventually?" Camilla frowned.

"Sure, sure." Conrad sounded so out of it that Camilla couldn't tell if he was being honest or not.

Nigel, Lance, and Darber soon departed the room, leaving Camilla with Conrad. The pair just sat there in awkward silence. Finally, Camilla asked, "Maybe it would be easier, to help give you cover, if I stayed in here with you."

"My personal Florence Nightingale?" Conrad asked with a drowsy grin. "Sure. I'd love to have you."

Camilla nodded. "Alright."

It was a short while before Camilla broke the silence again. "Thanks for letting me in on this."

"No problem." Conrad coughed. "You're not going to kick my ass after this, are you?"

Camilla smiled for the first time since the surgery began. "I think you know the answer to that."

———

THAT NIGHT, Nigel and Lance joined everyone for dinner, all except Conrad, who was conspicuously absent, and Tom, who still was laboring outside with the wood. Camilla helped Sarah cook dinner, with Carla occasionally joining in, though her attention remained with little Conrad.

Sarah in particular was chatting up a storm with Nigel, asking him what commodities and products still were available in town. She had not been off the homestead since she had arrived, and was eager to hear any kind of detailed news about what was going on in any community—any community that wasn't under the rule of thugs and mobsters.

Lance, for his part, kept quiet and ate. The young man was very polite and exchanged a few words with Liam, but otherwise didn't participate much in the conversation.

Just then, Tom strolled through the doorway from the kitchen. Sawdust covered his flannel jacket. "Hey everybody." He looked around. "So, where's Conrad?"

Camilla's skin burned. "He's not feeling well. He came down with something, a stomach bug probably."

Darber nodded. "He might be off his feet for a few days, if not a week or two. It all depends on how bad it is."

"Awwww." Carla, still holding little Conrad, looked at the baby and said, "Hear that? Grandpa's sick. We should make him a get well card."

"Really?" Tom raised an eyebrow. "Must have hit him pretty quick. He looked fine this morning."

"Well, sometimes a stomach bug can hit you without much warning," Darber said.

"No kidding. When I was trick-or-treating as a kid, I suddenly got so sick I puked on the sidewalk," Liam said.

Lance chuckled. "Yeah, when I was eight, I ate some bad chocolate from Halloween and spent two days in bed."

As the dinner drew to a close, Camilla turned to the plate of food sitting on the counter. She had prepared it separately and set it aside from the others. "I'll take this to Conrad."

"I hope," Lance began.

Camilla turned her head. Lance swallowed and shrank back in his chair. "I hope he feels better soon."

Camilla smiled. "Thanks."

———

CAMILLA CARRIED the plate down the hall to Conrad's door. She tapped on the door three times in close succession.

"Yeahlo," Conrad said. He clearly had meant to say "Yeah," but his tired voice slurred the word. Camilla opened the door and stepped inside.

Conrad lay in bed, dressed in nightclothes. A small candle on the end table provided some light.

He grasped a book on his lap. He probably had been reading it, but now was clearly too weak to read much more of it. Instead, he sat upright, just staring ahead through half-closed eyes.

"Din-din's here." Camilla smiled and raised the plate. "Broccoli, tomatoes, some mashed potatoes, and a little corn."

"Thanks." Conrad closed his book and set it off to the side. Camilla moved the candle to Conrad's dresser, then placed the plate on the end table. From there, she cut off a piece of broccoli and offered it to Conrad on a fork.

"I'm not that weak," Conrad said, "I can handle it."

"You look like you're going to keel over. C'mon, you need to eat as much of this as you can."

Conrad nodded. "Yes, ma'am." Then he ate the broccoli.

A few bites of broccoli and tomatoes later, Conrad asked, "So, they bought the story?"

"Ron really sold it. I don't think anyone's going to question a doctor." Camilla cut some more tomato. "So, did Nigel and Ron pack up everything?"

"Yep. And the smell is gone. We aired out the room. As far as anyone's concerned, I'm just an old codger with a bad case of stomach flu."

Camilla looked at Conrad's bandaged right arm. "As long as no one looks at your arm."

"I have plenty of long-sleeved shirts. I can cover that up," Conrad replied.

After feeding Conrad more tomato, Camilla remarked, "Still, don't you think you should tell Liam? He is your son."

Conrad sighed. "I want to. I probably should."

"So, what's the story?" Camilla asked.

Conrad hesitated. "I feel like something's going to happen soon. I don't know what. Maybe it won't be as bad as I'm fearing. But if it is, I figure Liam is going to want to be by my side."

"You don't want him near you when that happens," Camilla said.

Conrad shook his head. "There's no getting back what we could have had. If our world was peaceful, maybe we'd still enjoy twenty, thirty more years together. But he's a father now. He's got his own responsibilities, and he can't give them up for me. I'm not going to let him."

Camilla was about to cut more broccoli, but then she noticed only a small piece remained anyway. "I still think it's a damn shame you've been alone for so long without him."

Conrad reached out to Camilla, but his hand fell gently to his side. "This past year has felt like much longer than that. I'm almost forgetting what it's like to be alone."

Camilla fed Conrad the rest of his food.

RUBBING HIS HEAD, Liam walked down the hall.

Picking up some of the extra slack, including inspecting the grounds, had exhausted him. It was weird to have a night when he didn't join his father out on the back porch for a talk and maybe even a drink.

I should see him, Liam thought. But night had fallen hours ago. His dad was probably still in no shape to see anyone.

A set of rapid footsteps interrupted his train of thought. Camilla rushed from the hall intersection, clutching a bundle of rolled-up clothes. She was dressed in a long T-shirt that reached down to her thighs. Once she reached the door to his dad's bedroom, she opened it up and slipped inside without missing a beat.

Liam scratched his head. As far as he could remember, he never had seen Camilla go in and out of his father's bedroom late at night, and certainly not dressed so skimpily.

Should I really be that shocked? Liam turned around. Camilla and his dad had been involved in the past. Liam never had paid much attention to whether the two had gotten back together, but if it did happen, then so be it.

I can only wonder what those two are up to, he thought. A shiver ran down his spine. *On second thought....*

CHAPTER ELEVEN

TOM HELD out his hands close to the living room's crackling fireplace. "Central heating, eat your heart out," he said as he soaked up the flames' warmth. Beside him, Sarah laughed. "This might sound corny, but it actually feels better knowing I cut all this wood in the first place. If my dad were here, he'd say I'd have gone nuts."

Sarah wrapped an arm around Tom's. "He probably would have been shocked to hear you're a lumberjack now."

Tom shook his head. "You have no idea. He'd have never understood all this, living on a farm, cutting your own wood just for heat." He looked over his shoulder. Carla was playing with little Conrad on the couch, just beyond the shadow of the Christmas tree. Tom's smile faded. "It's still hard not to think of him. Christmas and Thanksgiving always brought us together until he passed. The family just drifted apart after that."

Sarah gripped him a little tighter. "That last Christmas wasn't so bad. We had each other."

"Yeah, and then about six months later, the whole world turned into something out of a *Mad Max* movie. Didn't see that coming," Tom replied.

Just then, the sound of jiggling bells cut through the air. Carla turned to her baby. "Hey. You hear that? I think Santa's coming! Here he comes! Here he comes!"

Indeed, a "fat" bearded man walked − or rather hobbled − through the hall doorway into the living room. He wore a big green robe with a pillow obviously padding out his abdomen, with a belt of round bells draped over his shoulder. Camilla followed beside him, followed by Liam, who was wearing an oversized floppy green hat.

"Merry Christmas!" Conrad bellowed in a deep baritone voice.

Sarah laughed. "Oh my God!"

Tom chuckled hard. Speaking proved to be a real challenge. "Hey, I thought Santa wore red."

Camilla patted "Santa" on the left shoulder. "We had to make do. We didn't have a red robe."

"Actually, in Great Britain, Santa does wear green. He's called Father Christmas over there," Conrad answered in his Santa voice.

Sarah then approached Liam. "So, what are you supposed to be?" she asked him.

"He's my elf!" Conrad replied loudly. Liam just smiled awkwardly and shrugged.

Carla held up little Conrad. "Look at the silly elf. Look at the silly elf!" Carla chirped. The baby just looked at Liam with a puzzled expression.

"Hey little feller," Conrad said, "You've been a good little boy this year?"

Carla raised little Conrad to just in front of her face, and then spoke in a high-pitched baby voice, "I haven't peed once on my parents today!"

"That's good to hear. Remember, Santa's always watching you," Conrad said.

"Would you like to hold me, Santa?" Carla asked, still in baby voice.

"Sure, but let Mrs. Claus help me to the couch. Santa's not as young as he used to be," Conrad said.

Camilla held on to Conrad's left arm and then gently braced him as the rancher sat on the couch. Camilla sat down beside him. "Okay," Conrad said, "Bring him here."

Carla handed little Conrad over to him. Conrad took the child.

———

As CONRAD PLAYED with his young namesake, Liam sat down next to Tom and Sarah on the floor. "Good job on the tree," Liam said.

"Thanks." Tom looked over Liam's shoulder at

Conrad. "Hey, I was just wondering. Do you think your dad's okay?"

"What do you mean?" Liam asked.

"I don't know. He's never looked the same since he got sick a few weeks ago. He just seems a little... weaker to me. And Camilla's always with him."

"I agree." Sarah turned her gaze to her former husband. "Don't you think something's up?"

Liam studied his father carefully. The pair had a point. His father moved much more slowly since he had taken ill, plus he rarely used his right hand. In fact, Liam never could recall his dad using both of his hands for anything since then. Also, Camilla accompanied his father around just about everywhere he went. Liam thought the closeness of the pair meant they had become more emotionally attached. But now that Liam thought about it, Camilla almost appeared to be nursing his father along.

"I hope he didn't pick up something horrible and he's just hiding it from us." Sarah sucked in a bitter breath. "It wouldn't shock me if your father is once again taking it all on his shoulders without telling us."

As much as Liam wanted to deny it, he admitted silently that his mother could be right. But what could his dad be hiding?

———

CONRAD HOBBLED BACK to his bedroom. "Oh, you were a delight," Camilla said as she followed him.

"Think so, huh?" Conrad asked as he opened the door of his bedroom.

The pair filed into the room. Conrad then let out an aching moan. "Damn." He plopped down hard on the bed.

Camilla undid Conrad's "Santa" robe and pulled it off him. "Tell me it wasn't that bad."

Conrad clutched his right arm. "I was doing okay at first, but the little guy's already getting big. He leaned against it, too much probably." He winced. "It is getting better. I swear to God. But it's taking its sweet time doing it."

Camilla brought Conrad his sling. He despised wearing it, but he needed to rest his arm. Reluctantly, he slipped his right arm inside.

Camilla sat down next to him. "It was nice, having everyone together. Seems like more and more we're all just spread out."

Conrad blew out a slow breath. "These are the good times." He looked to his window. "Once Christmas is over with, we're going to be back to thinking about what's going on out there."

"We haven't heard anything new about that army," Camilla said, "Maybe they're not going to make it here after all."

"Even if it is months or maybe a year or two, we can't take that chance," Conrad said. "You got to figure they're building up resources, getting stronger, extending their reach. We have to deal with this." He released his arm from the sling. "I just need a little more time. I'll be able to do what needs to be done."

"I hope so," Camilla said.

———

REG TRIED SLIPPING the ornament back on the Christmas tree, but the string once again slipped off the slender branch. Jeff, who was passing by but stopped near his friend, chuckled. "Forget it. It's amazing we haven't tossed this tree yet. Christmas has been over for six days."

"You know the rule, man." Reg relocated the ornament to a sturdy branch. "We don't take down the Christmas tree until New Year's is over."

"I would have kept it up until Arbor Day," Nigel said as he approached the pair.

He looked at the top of the tree. This school gym had been heavily adorned with Christmas decorations. Green holly and garlands lined the walls. Wreaths coated the main entrance doors. The left- and right-hand walls each had its own Christmas tree. Tonight, a few hundred of Hooper City's residents gathered here to ring in the new year.

"I hear you, Nigel." Reg backed up a step. "The city really needed this."

Nigel took a quick look around him. It was a testament to the efforts of Hooper City that people were provided for enough that they could spare the time to decorate the gym as well as other public places. He suspected the citizens were desperate for some kind of normalcy. True, electricity was not around to power Christmas lights, malls were not open to buy Christmas gifts, and no Christmas movies or television specials were available to watch.

But those things didn't make Christmas anyway. Nigel chuckled to himself, recalling the famous *Grinch* story from Dr. Seuss from when he was a child. *Who knew we'd actually live that tale?* he thought.

"Hey." Reg jabbed Nigel in the arm. "Take a look at that."

Nigel turned to the row of drink tables on the other side. Lance, close to one of them, was sipping a cup of apple cider. A young lady, perhaps eighteen or nineteen, was strolling over to him, with Lance as oblivious as could be. Judging from her long blonde hair and lightly tanned cheeks, Nigel easily could tell it was Tracy Lynn sidling up to Lance.

Tracy tapped Lance on the shoulder. The young man jolted, spilling some of his drink onto the floor.

Nigel winced. "Good God, kid," he said.

Lance turned around. Tracy laughed a little. Lance looked down, his cheeks reddening, then muttered something that Nigel and his friends couldn't make out. But then the two started exchanging more and more conversation.

"I'd have thought those two would have joined up by now," Nigel said.

"Speaking of joining up." Jeff walked past Nigel to

the other side of him. "You probably didn't hear, but Carmen's girl is pregnant."

"That so?" Nigel thought about the young men in town, the ones with spouses and partners.

Since he had risen to the town leadership, he had gotten to know many of the young men. Especially since they had to till the fields and produce crops for those who couldn't work, as well as help guard the harvests from thieves. And when he learned they were finding girlfriends, he began wondering about the possibility of new families in town. The aftermath of the solar event, plus the growing unease of the new military in the country, led a lot of people to opine that it was madness raising children in today's world.

"Hey!" Jeff pointed to a large clock on the wall. It was an old, wooden wind-up clock placed there a few months ago. The minute hand was two minutes before midnight. The new year was soon upon them.

"Okay! Everybody get ready for the big count-down!" Nigel clapped his hands as he walked to the center of the room. Jeff followed with a bottle of beer and a clean glass. Reg followed with two empty glasses.

The crowd quieted down. Jeff filled the glass with drink, then handed it to Nigel. The bait store owner turned town leader looked at everyone, feeling a bit hesitant of what to say. Speeches were not his forte. He had rarely even given toasts. But the times had changed, and so had he.

Nigel raised his drink. "To absent friends and

family. To the many, many people we lost through this horror. And...to the great hope we have for the future. If we make this work, if we live on and thrive, then we can say our tomorrow will be better than the yesterdays we endured. May God bless all of you!"

"Here! Here!" shouted many from the crowd as they raised their drinks in celebration.

Reg looked at the clock. "Almost time."

Nigel waved his drink. "Start it up for us, Reg."

Reg started the countdown. "Ten...nine...eight...seven...six...five...four...three...two...one!"

"Happy New Year!" shouted almost everyone in the hall. Many hugs and handshakes were exchanged. Before Lance could shake anyone's hand, Tracy pulled him into her embrace and kissed him passionately.

Nigel caught sight of it and laughed. Then he quickly refilled his drink. "Hey, it's an oldie, but I think the youngsters among us can follow." He then started off with the opening lines of "Auld Lang Syne."

The rest of the party joined in. And indeed, the rest of the night was just as merry.

———

LANCE STIRRED.

He awoke in the attic in which he slept with a slightly aching head. He barely remembered walking here from the party at the gym. Beside him, Tracy slept soundly. Lance pulled his covers down but not enough to fully expose his partner. She was so quiet. What had awakened him?

The attic of this store came with a glass window. There was a noise beyond, like a scratching. Lance was so caught up in rushing to the window that he hadn't thought to put on any clothes. Instead, he gazed out the window. But in the absence of any streetlights, he could make out nothing but the shadows of the nearby buildings. However, for a moment Lance thought he saw movement darting across the street.

Who could that be? Maybe one of the runners changing shifts? Even on New Year's Eve, the city's governing council insisted on some kind of watch patrol. It would make sense.

That must be it. Lance turned away, returning to the soft bed and the lovely woman sleeping there.

———

WHAT LANCE, or anyone else in Hooper City for that matter, didn't know was that the shape he had seen darting across the street belonged to a man who wasn't one of their own. Under the dark of night and while almost every soul in town slept soundlessly from a night of merrymaking, Sam crept out of Hooper City.

No one could have known Sam wasn't one of them unless a longtime denizen of the community took notice. Sam Keller was dressed in a flannel shirt, blue overcoat, and jeans. He kept his head down, did work for the town, and said little.

But that was all over now. Sam had completed his task, and was ready to report what he had found.

The young man did not slow his pace once he reached the snowy forest beyond the city limits. Instead, he pushed on until he reached a point where a ditch cut through the trees. He climbed down the shallow hill, then, as his feet hit the ground, he pulled out a handheld radio and flipped the red switch.

"Nest, this is Sparrow. I've taken flight. Estimate three days back to Nest without extraction. Threat level is low. Don't recommend extraction."

He waited until the radio buzzed. "Roger that, Sparrow," said a female voice, "Sum it up. How's it look?"

"It's better than we hoped," Sam replied. "They actually gathered and saved enough crops for winter. I've also gathered intel on several local ranches. They run along State Roads 29, 25 and 22."

"You know what to do from here on, Sparrow," the female voice said.

"Copy that," Sam said. He then switched off the radio.

He pulled out a notepad and a pen from his pocket. Making sure he chronicled all of his intelligence on paper was just as important as making it back to base. If something happened to him, at least there was a chance he could leave these notes on his person.

CHAPTER TWELVE

JOANNE DEADEN FLIPPED the radio switch off. Reclining in a folding chair, she stretched her arms. She almost had fallen asleep. However, receiving Sam's report had revitalized her.

She gazed at the small tent around her. Nothing but her sleeping bag and a duffel bag. Deaden had cared little for possessions, except for what she needed to survive and fight in a world that bared its ugly fangs. She even had forgotten it was New Year's Eve, except for the men outside expressing their wishes to make merry for the night.

Deaden stood up, then looked down at the green military uniform she had not yet changed out of. What was there to celebrate?

She yanked the tent flap open, exposing the world around her—a large camp of tents and flimsy metal sheds, with hundreds of civilians strewn about in sleeping bags or inside the shelters. Soldiers patrolled up and down aisles between the civilians, rifles carried openly, signs of tigers bearing their teeth.

Coughing and moaning cut through the air. The signs of the suffering. *Yeah, what a time to celebrate*, she thought bitterly.

"Move!" barked a familiar voice.

Deaden slowly turned her gaze to the path running up from the right-hand side. Gin approached, pointing his gun at a skinny man in dirty red and brown clothing. Matthew followed, wearing that same goofy-ass smile on his face as if the young, slender man had won a trip to Disney World. For his part, Gin remained the same movable mountain that he always was. The tall African man was rarely known to smile, yet Deaden never got the feeling he was brutish. Unfortunately, Deaden knew all too well that some of the soldiers under her command were less than gentlemanly. She had inflicted harsh punishment more than once because of it.

So, the question tonight was whether her troops had victimized this man, or was he actually the one doing the victimizing?

"Halt!" Gin shouted. The man in dirty clothing stopped, and then just as quickly tripped and fell to his knees.

"What's this?" Deaden asked.

"New Year's present, Cap!" Matthew said in his usual light French accent. The nearby portable light showed off his short blonde hair, even the red freckles on his cheeks, making him look more like a kid than ever.

Deaden's face hardened. "Name, now, and what's his offense?" She raised her chin. "Or is it *his* offense we're talking about here?"

"Ira Shimkus. Resident of Redmond," Gin said, "You interviewed him personally."

Deaden turned to the trembling man. "Right. A mob operator, or so some of your fellow cohorts confessed."

Ira coughed. "I didn't do anything," he said softly. Deaden suspected Ira's men had gotten to this man first before he was brought to her for discipline.

"He got a little horny with a woman," Matthew said with a toothy grin. "Everyone around heard ya. Six witnesses told us about it, saying the woman was there in the tent with her boobies hanging out."

"Enough, Corporal," Deaden said wearily. "Be professional when you speak."

"The witnesses told the same story. We interviewed them separately," Gin said, betraying not a hint of satisfaction or glee in his tone. "There is no question this man assaulted the woman."

Deaden balled her right hand into a fist. "Well, it sounds like you're every bit the scumbag that your so-called friends said you were."

"Finks!" Ira said, quaking even more. "Damn them! You Nazis killed Laird, you tortured the rest!"

He was cut off when Matthew suddenly shoved the nose of his rifle inches from Ira's face. "Hey. My great granddaddy died fightin' the Nazis, buddy. You keep callin' us that, and I'll blow your brains all over the dirt."

"Frankly, I don't care much what you did before we met, provided you were willing to cooperate." Deaden leaned a little closer, while digging through her right pants pocket. "It's one hell of a problem when you disappoint me."

Then she ripped her fist free of her pocket and slammed Ira in the face.

The former mob flunky hit the ground in a screaming fit. A tooth flew out and hit the ground nearby. Deaden raised her hand, which now was adorned with soft metal bracing. It wasn't as hard as brass knuckles, but it provided Deaden's punch with an added kick that would get across her point well enough.

Matthew let out a joyful holler. "Let me do the punishing, Captain." He pointed his gun at the writhing Ira. "I'm going to blow off his balls."

"Stow it, Corporal," Deaden said. "I'm more old-fashioned. Gin, the chains."

Gin nodded. He turned and barked to a pair of African men patrolling by Deaden's tent, then spoke in a language Deaden wasn't familiar with. Yet, within minutes, the two men returned with manacles and chains. Deaden was proud of the efficiency that Gin and the men directly under him had showed, even if only Gin spoke English adequately enough.

Ira looked up, blood trickling from his mouth and

nose. "Wha?" he asked pathetically. He suddenly was assaulted by the two men, who bound his arms and legs with the manacles.

"I should execute you right here and now, but you have working hands and legs. That means you can push and pull, or dig and plant. So, consider yourself my personal slave. You're going to work for us until you die, or I become merciful and reduce your sentence." Deaden then paused for effect, to make Ira think about it. "I would not bet on the later."

"You're the Captain's bitch," one of Gin's men said with a laugh.

Deaden scowled, but said nothing to rebuke him, feeling he would not understand her words anyway. Deaden had experienced enough trouble trying to pull this army together in a way in which those who understood English and their country's native tongue could filter orders down to those soldiers who couldn't speak more than a few English words. "Just get him away from me," she said.

Gin translated for the two men. Then they seized Ira and dragged him away.

"Going soft, Captain." Matthew chuckled. "These American assholes deserve some proper dis-uh-pleen." He then raised his rifle at the departing Ira and made mock shooting sounds.

"American assholes?" Gin glowered at Matthew. "The captain is American. Many of the men are American."

"Oh." Matthew lowered his gun. "Sorry. Forgot myself for a moment."

Forgot himself, Deaden thought with disdain. She also couldn't forget that many of the foreign soldiers in her company had little respect for the land they now inhabited, or its people. They had been told that restoring America was essential to returning the world to a modicum of stability and modernity, yet some of them had no problems exploiting the country's sorry state. Corporal Matthew Francois had not shown himself to be a discipline case, yet Deaden couldn't shake her unease about the man.

One of these days I might find myself with a knife shoved in my back, she thought.

She sighed. "Reconvene the command staff at oh six hundred for deployment instructions."

"We're moving out?" Gin asked.

"Sam's got valuable intel. He's headed our way. I think we might finally solve some of our supply problems," Deaden said, "You two get some rest. Your duty shift ended ten minutes ago."

"Suits me." Matthew yawned mockingly. "Time to hit the hay." He rushed off down the dirt path, but then turned around and said, "Oh, Captain! Happy New Year." Matthew snickered, then left.

Deaden shook her head. At least she was free of Matthew's asshatery until morning. She turned to Gin and said, "Good night, Corporal."

"Good night, Captain." Gin nodded, then walked away.

As Deaden's fingers grazed her tent flap, she stopped to watch Gin leave. "I wonder who the hell I can trust around here," she whispered.

―――――

LIAM LET OUT a huff as he shut the door behind him. "Goodbye, Christmas. Finally!" he said with a laugh. The last of the Christmas garlands had been cleared out. "And it only took, what, until the end of January?" he asked himself.

He couldn't blame everyone. It was hard to let go of the Christmas tree and the festive decorations, but eventually his dad put his foot down and told everyone it was time to clear out the living room. At first, Liam figured his father simply wanted to get things back to normal, but he also began wondering if the decorations distracted him. Since Liam started taking down the holly, the garlands and the ornaments, he noticed his dad withdrawing again. His mom also kept her distance more from her onetime husband.

He stepped through the living room. *It's like this isn't a home so much anymore*, he thought. *It's more like an apartment where everyone just waves "Hi!" on the way to work.* He frowned. He didn't like it. Perhaps because he had lived so long without his dad, and then tasted having his family under one roof again, the added distance between his parents nagged at him.

That irritation only received a boost when his

mother wandered into the living room. She walked slowly, and peeked around the corner before proceeding farther into the room. Liam's skin itched. What was she doing?

"Hi Mom." He spoke loudly, on purpose.

Sarah raised her head. "Oh! Liam!" She clutched her chest. "Wow, you gave me a scare. I didn't know you were standing there."

"I guess I'm a regular ninja," Liam said, though he couldn't smile at his own joke. "So, what are you doing? You look a little on edge."

"I'm fine. Say, where's your father?"

"Outside, doing exercises with Camilla." Liam pointed his thumb to the closed front door. "He doesn't expect to be back inside for most of the day."

Sarah let out a soft breath. "Well, good for him. At his age, he needs all the exercise he can get." She stretched her arms. "Now, when you say 'exercises,' do you mean jogging, or bike riding?"

"Well, I think running and ducking is part of it," Liam said.

Sarah's smile faded. "Ah. Guess by 'exercise,' Conrad means military exercises. Dodging gunfire, things like that."

"You know what's coming, Mom. Dad would be stupid not to get ready for it, especially after that nasty cold he had."

Sarah turned away. "Your dad can't expect anything but war, can he?"

Liam caught his mother before she wandered out

of the room into the kitchen. "Mom, is there a problem with you and Dad?"

Sarah stopped and tilted her head back. "You mean the usual, or something new?" She sounded like she was joking, but Liam wasn't buying it.

"C'mon Mom, this isn't funny. You're giving him a wide berth. What's going on?"

Sarah, now fully turned in her son's direction, smiled awkwardly. "Guess I just have a lot on my mind. If this new army does show up, I just wonder what your father will do about it, and what he'll ask all of us to do."

"I don't get it. Ask us to do what, defend ourselves? We'd do that anyway."

"Liam, what if these people aren't as bad as what your father thinks? What if it's okay for us to go with them? Haven't you wondered if maybe someday we can go home?"

"But Mom, we're home now."

"Not here. I mean home in Redmond. Home where we used to live. Okay, maybe not our actual house. God knows if there's anything left of it now. I'm just wondering if we could have a normal life again. What if they have working washing machines, dryers, air conditioners, something other than farm and country?"

Liam frowned. "What are you saying? You hate it here?"

"No!" Sarah raised her hands. "No, absolutely not. With all that happened, I couldn't be more grateful to be here and not running for my life on the city streets or..." Her voice trailed off. "...being locked up by horrid, evil gangsters."

She leaned up against the back wall near the kitchen doorway. "I just want to know that this can change, that things can get better. I don't think your dad feels the same way. In fact, I know he doesn't. He's never been able to. Sometimes he gets scary when he acts that way." Her eyes met Liam's. "Do you think if I wanted to leave he would let me?"

"I'm sure he would, but why not stay here with us, with me and little Conrad?"

"I know, I know. I haven't decided. I don't know whose this army is. That's why I want to find out. And, if they can help us, I want to know I can leave without your father forcing me."

Liam blinked his eyes quickly. He wasn't expecting to hear this. His mother was thinking of leaving? This was insane. "Mom, I'm sure Dad wouldn't stop you, but I think it's crazy to want to leave. I mean, we're all together again. Finally! I only could dream of this! Who cares if they have a few working appliances or lights or whatever? I'd trade all of that to have my mom and dad back. This is what I want, and you should want it too."

Sarah cringed. "Liam, I want to be with you."

"But you don't want to be with Dad."

Sarah tilted her head away. "You know we went our separate ways. I think fondly of him as a good friend, but..."

"It doesn't matter to you either way. I guess that's it." Liam's face twisted into a scowl. "Fine. But at least this time you can make the choice without involving me."

He turned around, and now it Sarah's turn to stop him from leaving. "Wait a minute! What do you mean by that?"

Liam spun around, the temperature rising in his cheeks. "C'mon, Mom. You really had to get sole custody of me? Not even tell me where he lived, give me any hope I could have him in my life again? Hell, I had to spend years trying to track him down. So, yeah, this time it's all on you. You want to stay or go, at least now you're not dragging me along with you."

He couldn't take it. His hand flew to the door and yanked it open. "I need to go outside for a bit." He vanished out the door without giving his mother another look, to gauge what kind of damage he might have done by his words.

CHAPTER THIRTEEN

NIGEL CHUCKLED. "Is that arm still giving you trouble?"

"Screw off, Nigel." Conrad realized he had been cradling his right arm for longer than he had intended. Yet, it was hard to stop holding it, if only to mitigate the persistent ache he had been feeling since arriving in Nigel's store.

"Guess Doctor Ron took off part of your funny bone while he was at it," Nigel said as he led Conrad through the doorway to the back room of the store.

Conrad took the opportunity, with Liam being gone, to shove his arm back in the sling under his coat. Father and son recently had arrived in Hooper City for another bartering run. Liam had parted to do a little shopping of his own, and Conrad eagerly allowed the young man his space. It also gave Conrad time to nurse his damaged arm without his son asking questions. "The damn thing sure is taking its time to heal."

"All kidding aside, I'm glad you made the trip," Nigel said as he circled a wooden bench. The back room was meant to be a small storage area for the store, but Nigel recently had added a small bench for resting and socializing, especially when sensitive information was discussed.

"I was going to radio you this evening, but I might as well tell you now. I was on the horn with someone last night. He ran into someone fleeing from up north. He had the whole story on our mysterious new military that's trucking across the country."

Conrad nodded. "Is that right?"

"Yeah." Nigel placed a cup of apple cider on the table by the bench. "Sorry it's not the Texas bourbon I promised. Turns out I got a bum lead on that."

"I'd rather not be drinking right now." Conrad picked up the cider with his free hand and drank.

"Anyway, this man, Jesse's his name, he used to live in the Chicago suburbs. He got to witness firsthand what was going on in his neck of the woods. He lived in one of the refugee camps for a time. Some of the folks there resided far east. Jesse gathered a lot of info, and he told it to my guy Willard."

Conrad relaxed on the bench while Nigel spoke.

"This is how the story goes. A couple of army units scattered around the hemisphere still had working vehicles, mostly boats, after the sun fried all the electronics. They set out to find one another, but it was very slow going. Along the way, they picked up units from other countries, European, South and Central American, some African. Not many Asian units, but a couple of survivors from Taiwan said the aftermath over there was pretty damn ugly."

"Didn't want to give specifics, huh?" Conrad asked.

"No," Nigel said. "Anyway, a month ago the army finally came together. They called themselves the ALA, or America's Liberation Army. But it's really a hodgepodge of a bunch of countries in one. Willard called it a regular chimera."

"Chimera?" Conrad asked.

"It's part dragon, part lion, part goat. You know, a monster that's a whole bunch of animals in one. Something out of the Greek myths and all that. Anyway, that's kind of like what this army is. About a third of the soldiers don't speak English, and about a fifth speak it very badly. They don't have enough translators to go around, so it's a bitch to get the army to work efficiently."

"But they're working pretty good now if they're swarming all over the country," Conrad said.

"Yeah, and it's a problem for us. The level-headed folks are taking on the cities. They figure since the cities are more reliant on supply chains for food and water, it's easier to take those places. But out here in the countryside, it's a different story. I wouldn't call it paradise here, but we have managed to get on our feet, at least as far as survival goes. The ALA figure we're more likely to cause a ruckus if they try to tell us what to do, so we get the meanest SOBs out of the lot."

"In other words, they crush folks like us, so we don't squeal," Conrad said.

Nigel pointed to Conrad. "Damn right."

"So, what's the story with the actual U.S. government? If they're not in charge anymore, who's running this ALA?" Conrad asked.

"The President was at Camp David when the EMP hit. He did make it back to Washington, but by then the breakdown in the city was bad. It was basically a small civil war up and down the East coast until the beginning of winter." Nigel sighed.

"Jesse didn't know all the details, but he said even if the president, any of his cabinet, or anyone in Congress survived, not a one of them has any real power anymore. The ALA is run by a small council of officers, and God knows if they're looking out for anyone but themselves. According to Jesse, discipline isn't exactly an ALA priority, and some soldiers have been dishing out brutal punishment on the streets."

Conrad nodded. "As my Uncle Josh would say, 'Now we know the lay of the land.'"

"Well, it seems as though the lie is that these people want to help us out. If they're truly running a relief effort, they'd work hand in glove with us, instead of trying to crush us with an iron fist." Nigel shook his head.

"But that's not the worst of it. Willard confirmed

that they're coming this way. They came in from the north, then overran Redmond and Wynwood, and now they're curving back in this direction. Now, if they're taking Interstate 80, that will lead them to State Road 22 soon, if they haven't taken it already. Hooper City will be in their crosshairs in a few days."

"But my home will be even closer," Conrad added grimly.

"I know." Nigel shook his head. "I wish I could say you have nothing to worry about, but these guys are fanning out to get even the folks who are living off the grid. Still, you could pick up and make a run for it. It's still easy to overlook a small group hiding out in the country."

"Start all over again? Where? Nigel, I've got a small grandbaby who needs a home. Do I drag my little one out there among the feral animals, the numbing cold, the ticks or mosquitoes or whatever the hell is lurking in the weeds or the forest or the rivers?" Conrad braced his still weak arm. "Besides, it's all I can do to rebuild my strength. I don't know if I can take on the world like I used to do."

The rancher sighed. "Besides, Sarah isn't convinced this army is a bunch of bad apples. If they show up at my front door, she might want to go with them. I even could lose Ron. I know he's been through a lot, given a lot for me. But I can tell he's wishing for something better than just holing up at a ranch with just a few people, no town, no community." Conrad exhaled loudly. "Damn."

"You afraid Liam and Carla will leave?" Nigel asked.

"Not really. I've talked with those two. They know the risks if they leave and they don't want to go for it, especially with little Conrad. If this group is run by a bunch of real fascists, they might take the baby away and raise him to be one of their little zombified henchmen."

Nigel stared off into space. "Not something I'd ever imagine would happen here."

Conrad raised his nearly empty cup of cider. "Few people do." Then he drank the rest.

————

CONRAD SLOWED his pace once again. "You okay, Dad?" Liam asked.

"What? Oh, sure. Just a little tired." Conrad picked up speed, but he figured it wouldn't last. Greater fatigue was turning out to be a regular feature of life for him, despite his efforts to build up his strength. But since they had been on their feet for the past three hours, at least he had a fair excuse.

I used to pedal a bike all the way to Wynwood, Conrad thought. *I wonder if I could handle a bicycle that way again?* He was becoming way too conscious of his shortcomings, and he hated it. Better to change the subject.

"So, find anything surprising for your boy?"

Conrad asked, injecting as much cheer into his voice as he could.

"What?" Liam asked.

"C'mon, you pestered the hell out of me to go to Hooper City with me, so I figured you wanted to get your son something good."

"Oh." Liam put his hands in his jeans pockets. "Well, I did find something, but it wasn't for little Conrad."

"Well, spill it already." Conrad laughed. "When you get quiet, I get worried."

Shaking his head, Liam pulled out a gold ring with a sparkling diamond gem. Conrad stopped in his tracks and grabbed Liam by the wrist, hoisting the ring by the old man's face.

"Son of a bitch," Conrad said, "This is what I think it is?"

Liam swallowed before answering. "It is. It is, very much."

Conrad laughed loudly. "Well, if my eyes and ears don't deceive me, I think you're finally going to pop the question!"

Liam yanked the ring back. "Dad, it's not like that. I mean, it's not what you think."

"What's wrong?" Conrad asked, "You got something on your mind."

Liam sighed. "This...this might sound stupid. I'm scared to do this."

"Well, it's natural for a man to feel scared before asking someone for their hand. Although in your case, you kind of skipped over that step into the whole family life thing, so I'd think it'd be much easier now."

"I thought it would be, too." He sighed. "I don't know. I keep thinking about you and mom. I had a little dustup with mom a few days ago, and it just brought up a bunch of bad feelings."

Conrad put his hand on Liam's shoulder. "The divorce. That's what this is all about."

Liam nodded. "I didn't even know I had that stuff boiling inside me until I let it all loose on Mom. Damn."

"And you're worried that you and Carla might suffer a similar fate?"

"I don't think it'll end that way for me and Carla. I love her. I'd die for her, her and my son. But when I think of marrying her, I get these jitters. I don't want to do anything wrong. I don't want to mess up."

"Mess up like I did," Conrad added.

"No, not you," Liam said, "It was Mom who made up those stories about you, trashed you to get rid of you. This is her fault."

"Now hold on there." Conrad released Liam's shoulder. "I'm not going to deny that she hurt me mightily. But I can't stand here as God is my witness and say I was an angel in that household. I didn't do my best. Maybe we still would have split up. I guess we were both too different in our guts. But that's not how you and Carla are. The way you two act around each other is like..."

Liam smiled. "Like what?"

Conrad shook his head. "Something really good. Just ran out of metaphors there. Grant an old man his foibles. The point is that you're in the best shape I've seen a man with his lady to get hitched. I don't believe your marriage is going to crash and burn like mine and your mother's."

Liam looked at the ring in his hand, then at Conrad. "Thanks."

Conrad grabbed Liam's shoulder again. "No problem. Now, how about we get going. I don't want to be caught out in the dark before we hit the ranch. And you've got to rehearse your wedding proposal." He started walking. "Now, if you want to ask me, I got some pointers that will make it sound lovely and flowery. She'll melt in your arms."

"I think I'll ask Mom first," Liam said as he put the ring in his pocket.

"The hell you say," Conrad deadpanned.

Up ahead, a rusted, battered sign with a "22" against a dingy green shield emerged into view. "Almost home," Conrad said with a happy sigh.

"Looking forward to checking the chickens?" Liam asked.

"Maybe," Conrad said, though it was more likely he would collapse into bed not long after crossing the threshold. Camilla likely would fix him some soup and bring it to him.

Food brought to his room. Conrad bristled at the thought. It was like he was turning into an invalid.

His condition wasn't nearly as bad as his father's when he had deteriorated, but the thought still terrified him.

As soon as they passed the sign, a lone figure quickly approached them from behind. "Hello," the man said. Conrad and Liam stopped and turned around. The traveler, dressed in a flannel shirt under a heavy coat, walked up to them surprisingly fast.

"Afternoon," Conrad said, a little wary. He fished his left arm down toward the gun on his belt. He didn't care to be so suspicious, but nowadays it was rare to bump into somebody on the road.

The man was now close enough that Conrad and Liam easily could check his features. The man was young, clean shaven, with a cap covering a head of red hair. The traveler raised his hand, showing off a folded-up piece of paper. "This is for you. Just consider me the mailman."

He shoved it near Liam's chest. The younger Drake quickly snatched it. Conrad spoke, "What's this about?" However, the man simply smiled and dashed off.

"What the hell..." Liam quickly opened the paper. He and his father read the paper.

"Shit," Conrad said in a near whisper.

———

THE SCREEN DOOR FLEW OPEN. Conrad stormed through the living room. Camilla and Sarah were

already in the kitchen when the rancher marched by
the open doorway.

"Hey," Camilla said, "what's got your ass on fire?"

Conrad spun around, his eyes ablaze. Then he
passed the paper to Camilla. She took it and read it.
"We'll be coming to your home in the morning.
Please prepare to receive us. Sincerely, Captain
Joanne Deaden of the American Liberation Army."

Sarah gasped. "That's the military you told us
about?"

Conrad gritted his teeth. "Damn straight. Nigel
told me all about them, and then all of a sudden
someone on the road just hands me the letter like he
was giving out mail from the postal service?"

"How in God's name did he know you lived here?"
Camilla asked.

Conrad threw up his left arm. "Who the hell
knows? The bastards could have been watching us
come and go. They sent out a scout to nail us just
before we got home."

At that moment, Tom stepped into the room
from the side door, his shirt coated with snow. "Hey."
Then he spotted Conrad. "Welcome back. Trip went
okay?"

"Question." Conrad glared at him. "Did you ever
see any visitors outside while you were out on
patrol?"

"What?" Tom asked.

"Focus, man. We just got invited to a get together,
courtesy of the American Liberation Army, and I

think the invitation's mandatory. They know about this house and that we live here. So, I'm asking you if you spotted anybody taking a gander at the farm."

"Conrad, if I had seen somebody, I sure as hell would have told you," Tom replied with indignation.

"You sure you're remembering correctly?" Conrad advanced one step on him. "Might want to refresh that noggin of yours."

"Conrad, stop it!" Sarah rushed to Tom and got between them. "What the hell is wrong with you?"

"What is wrong is that I think we're being spied on," Conrad said.

"Yeah, they probably just passed by, saw the house, and wanted to make sure we knew they were coming. That's called being polite," Sarah said.

"That was being polite back in the days when people weren't coveting the very land you lived on," Conrad said.

"No kidding," Camilla added. "We've already had two mobs try stealing this place."

"And these people haven't done that. Think about it! Why didn't they come in with guns blazing?" Sarah said, waving her hands.

"Negotiating terms of surrender is preferable to wasting your ammo," Conrad said.

Sarah cringed. "God. You are absolutely impossible. So, what are you going to do? Spend all night burying more mines out in the lawn? Maybe you stowed away a nuclear bomb?"

Conrad pushed back his coat, revealing the gun

on his holster. "I will receive them properly, as a gentleman. And if they don't behave accordingly, I will have to eject them from my property."

Camilla smiled. "Need some help?"

Conrad started for the hall. "Madame, if you please."

But before Conrad could leave the living room, Sarah jumped in the way. "Okay. Fine. Do what you must. But if they come in for coffee and snacks, I will talk to them. You can't stop me from talking to them."

Conrad nodded once. "Do as you like, Sarah. I've never been able to stop you from doing otherwise."

CHAPTER FOURTEEN

THEY WERE COMING.

Conrad backed off from the eyepiece. This periscope, looking out from the attic window, was the closest thing the old rancher possessed to an early warning system since he lost his electronics. A tall, spindly woman marched down State Road 22 in front of ten other soldiers in a wedge formation. All of them sported green army fatigues and were armed with handguns in holsters, and many of them carried rifles over their shoulders.

They'll be paying us a visit, Conrad thought. He reached for the belt and holsters on the metal box behind him. "Guess I shouldn't disappoint," he said.

———

CONRAD WAITED for his guests out by the side of the road. About ten minutes had passed. He purposely waited by the heavy bushes that draped over the dirt onto the asphalt. The foliage would conceal him until the soldiers were about eight feet away.

Sure enough, the female soldier leading the pack raised her hand when she and her party got to about that distance. Conrad leisurely stepped out into full view, his boots hitting the surface of the road. "Good morning," he said, "You all out practicing maneuvers today? Or do they call it something else now?"

The female soldier frowned as if puzzled, but then composed herself and spoke, "Conrad Drake, is it?" She started her approach once again, with her men close behind. "You must have received our message. I'm glad to see we don't alarm you."

"If you're planning to pass by peacefully, of course you don't," Conrad replied.

"If by pass by, you mean visit and discuss the future of yourself and your household, then absolutely," she said.

Now Deaden had closed to gap to just a couple of feet. *This lady's tall*, Conrad thought. Her brown hair was cut short, but not very, as it still dangled over her shoulders. She still appeared feminine enough, but gave off such an icy attitude that, combined with her imposing height, she indicated she would be a tough customer.

"Our future's just fine. Captain Joanne, I take it?" Conrad asked.

"Captain Deaden." The army leader came to a

halt, her gaze almost even with Conrad's. "That is how I'm properly addressed, Mister Drake."

"Too bad. Joanne's a fine name," Conrad said.

Captain Deaden ignored Conrad's comment and instead turned an eye to the fallen trees. "Looks like you had some tree problems. What happened? Diseased trunks? Storm risk? Funny, I don't see any trunks around here. Of course, you could have dug them up, but I get the feeling you wouldn't waste that kind of time with all your crops to take care of."

Conrad kept his gaze on the captain. "They're like my personal doormen. Bertha and Goliath. They keep out unwanted visitors, especially ones that drive heavy automobiles and come armed to the teeth."

"Very clever. You sound like someone who's a good study on disaster survival. Perhaps we can work together."

Conrad fought to keep his eyes from rolling. "Work together, or do you mean working for you? There's a difference, Captain. I pay attention to how people talk to me."

Deaden pivoted away from the trees, back to the rancher. "So, what are you looking for, Mister Drake?"

"Lay your cards on the table. Tell me what you want. Then, I want you and the ten smiling faces behind you to leave my property and never come back." He glanced at Deaden's soldiers. Not a single one of them cracked a smile. *Figures*, he thought.

"Well, I can't promise you the latter, but I will be

happy to tell you what I want from you," Deaden said.

Conrad's throat clenched. A threat was implied there, that's for sure. "Fine. I'll escort you to my home, provided you leave your weapons out here," he said.

A few of the men chuckled, but Deaden waved her hand. "That's fine."

"Captain?" asked one of the soldiers, a young man with short blonde hair and a French accent.

"Do it," she said. "We're not enemies here, after all."

You don't buy that, and I know it, Conrad thought. But he kept his composure.

———

CONRAD OPENED THE FRONT DOOR, then the screen door. "Welcome." He walked quickly, to get Deaden inside, and then shut the door. He insisted the men stay outside. Deaden agreed easily. The captain was very confident Conrad wasn't some lunatic who'd try something.

Maybe she's got no fear in her veins, Conrad pondered. *Or maybe she figures she's got nothing to lose. Let's face it, this world has taken a shitload from everybody who's survived it, filed them down to their cores. I wonder if this lady always had been a soldier before this mess.*

A plate of corn, potato salad and cut meat lay on the table by a glass of water. "We prepared a meal for you," Conrad said. "We figured you'd appreciate some home cooking after a long march from wherever you've been."

Deaden nodded. "Thank you." She sat on the couch near the food. "I just came from a refugee camp about fifty miles south of here. The people are from all over, Davies, Wynwood, Redmond..."

Conrad leaned forward. Deaden stopped in mid-sentence, then said, "I see that caught your interest."

"You could definitely say that," Conrad said, "I had some recent...dealings in those places."

Deaden jabbed a piece of meat with the fork. "Then you can imagine the state some of those people are in. Surviving vandals, mobs, gangs. Davies was under the thumb of a local dictator who, rumor has it, was killed." Then she took a big bite.

"No rumor, Captain. He's very much dead," Conrad said.

"Well, the town experienced a terrible riot in its north end when those rumors hit. Fortunately, we pacified it and took in the survivors."

Pacified. Another word he didn't like hearing from this lady.

"With the food and medicine on hand, we've been able to pull many of them from death's door. But at least half of them are very productive. We need more assistance, and we can't afford to spread our forces too thin."

"Well, if you like to barter, hell, maybe some donations, so be it." Conrad spread out his hands.

"You're a man who knows his civic duty. I like that," Deaden said, "But the situation is desperate. Mere donations aren't going to do. I need...direct control of your homestead's resources."

Conrad kept still, not betraying his thoughts.

"Relocating you and your family to the camp would be the best option," Deaden said. "We've been gathering survivors under our protection."

"From cities that are all burned out and ruined. I can see that. But we're fine here," Conrad said.

"Yes, but we have working electronics. Not a lot, but enough to help with medicine, air conditioning..."

"And way too many people to be effective for us. We'd be in long lines for that stuff," Conrad said. "We know how to work this land and provide for ourselves, and we've done well so far in bartering for things we don't have."

Just then, Sarah pushed open the hall door, stopping Deaden from replying. "Conrad, is this our company?" She sounded mildly irritated.

Conrad rose. "Just wanted to get the good captain settled in here." He turned to Deaden. "Captain Joanne Deaden, this is Sarah Sandoval."

Sarah extended her hand. "Hi. Nice to meet you."

Deaden took it and shook it once, firmly. "Thank you, Sarah." Then she released it. "I've been curious about the kinds of people living under this roof. I'd like to know how much you know about the outside and what's available to you."

Sarah's smile grew. "I've been hoping things have been getting better."

"I think they are, or can be. That's why I'm here," Deaden said. "We've been taking back land, city by city, town by town, but it's not easy, and we've suffered delays." She leaned a little closer in Sarah's direction. "If I could, I'd like to talk to you privately."

"Excuse me?" Conrad asked.

"In your house, of course," Deaden added. "Any room will be fine."

"Anything you need to say to her can be said in front of me, Captain," Conrad said sternly.

"Conrad, I don't think this is a problem," Sarah said.

"Well, it is for me," Conrad said. "You think I'm leaving you alone with her?"

"Mister Drake, if you fear for her safety, I assure you I have better things to do than to threaten someone in your house. Particularly since I'm the only one of my company inside and you have the advantage of numbers," Deaden replied.

Conrad advanced one step toward his guest, taking the opportunity to overshadow her since she remained seated. "The point, Captain, is that I don't need anything said in confidence to a member of my household that I don't know about."

"Conrad, I will talk to Captain Deaden without you, either here or outside with her. You can choose," Sarah said in a flat but firm tone.

Conrad sucked in a loud breath, then answered

his ex. "Liam. He comes in and sits with you. That's my terms."

Sarah nodded. "That's fine."

"Liam? Is that the young man walking with you the other day?" Deaden asked.

"Yes, he is," Conrad replied curtly.

"My son. Mine...and his," Sarah added gently.

"Oh." Deaden raised an eyebrow. "You two are married?"

"Were," Conrad quickly corrected.

Deaden stirred her up her last bit of potato salad. "I see. That doesn't come as a terrible surprise. Sure, you may bring in your son."

Conrad stood up. "I'll bring him in." He opened his hall door and hollered, "Liam! Get your ass in here!"

Sarah dropped her head in her open hands. "God, Conrad!"

———

CAMILLA SAT by Conrad in his bedroom while the rancher flipped up a loose wooden panel to reveal a telescope and a wire with an ear bud hanging from it. "Sorry I don't have another for you, but I didn't figure I'd have more than one person with me when something bad went down."

"Did you rig all the rooms like this?" Camilla softly chuckled.

"No, just the living room." Conrad leaned into the

telescope, then turned the focus knob. The image of Captain Deaden on the couch with Sarah and Liam came into sharp focus.

"I put in this scope about twelve years ago. Figured that if the living room was breached for any reason, I could sneak in here and get a good look at what's going on." He planted the bud in his right ear. "There we go. Yeah, our lady captain thinks she's smart as hell. Well, she's in for quite a surprise."

"Okay, just remind me, you're not scared she's going to take Sarah or Liam hostage, right?" Camilla asked.

"No, I don't figure her for that, but she could talk Sarah into something, going with her, trying to peel Liam away. Some of these people study brainwashing techniques, the art of mental manipulation."

"You once told me no man could convince Sarah to do anything even if they held a gun to her head," Camilla said with a chuckle.

"Yeah. That's the problem." Conrad tightened the focus a little more. "That's a woman in there. Ah, she's talking." He leaned in a little closer.

———

DEADEN HAD PULLED OUT A NOTEPAD, which now rested on her lap. She scribbled quickly as she spoke, while Liam sat right next to his mother, eyeing the woman with distrust. The army captain seemed to ignore him completely. "Sarah Sandoval," she said, "native born?"

"Second generation. My mom's parents came from Honduras. My dad's mom was born in Cuba, married a farmer in the northern part of the state," Sarah replied.

Deaden kept her gaze on the pad, still writing as she talked. "I'm third generation. I had great-grandparents who emigrated from the Netherlands. Running from the Nazis. So, how long have you been living here?"

Sarah tilted her head back. "Oh, about nine months maybe. It's so hard to keep track of time anymore. I know it was summer when I...I was rescued and brought here."

"Rescued?" Deaden asked.

"Conrad and my boyfriend, Tom, they came after me. I was taken away by a bunch of thugs. They worked for a crime boss in the city I lived in."

"Which was?" Deaden questioned further.

"Redmond," Sarah replied.

"Was this crime boss Marcellus Maggiano?" Deaden asked.

Sarah straightened up. "That's right. You know about him?"

"I thoroughly interviewed the survivors of Redmond. I know a lot about what went on there." Deaden cleared her throat. "So, did you suffer any personal abuse or trauma during your captivity?"

Sarah's face twitched. "It was...degrading. I'll say that."

"Did you suffer any abuse of a physical or sexual nature?" Deaden asked.

"Okay, I think that's enough," Liam cut in, "Mom went through a lot. That's all you need to know."

Deaden still didn't look up from her notes. "I need to properly understand what you and your family have gone through, Mister Drake." Now she looked up. "We have a lot of ways to treat people who have been through all sorts of horrible things. Your mother needs to know that those choices are available."

"Liam, it's okay," Sarah said softly.

Liam settled back in the couch. Deaden put her pen back to paper. "Go on," the captain said.

"I was forced to strip several times," Sarah said with an evident lump in her throat. "No, they didn't... they didn't rape me. But I was felt up more than once."

"Do you suffer from nightmares, adverse health conditions, or sudden flashes of memory?" Deaden asked.

"No. Actually, I've been doing quite well. I've been settling into my new life nicely."

Deaden looked up. "Well, that's good to hear. But I am curious about why you and Conrad are no longer together."

Sarah pushed back into the couch. "Well, that was a long time ago. Probably going on thirty-one years."

"That long? I must say, it's quite interesting that you've chosen to live under the same roof as your ex-husband. I trust you two have an amicable relationship," Deaden said.

Sarah smiled, though a bit awkwardly. "We've learned to live with each other."

"Was the initial separation acrimonious?" Deaden asked.

Sarah drew in her legs. "It was far from ideal."

"Did you suffer any physical or mental abuse? Were you being cheated on?" Deaden asked.

"Okay, put on the brakes, Cap!" Liam stood up. "Nothing like that happened and you don't need to ask Mom about it anymore."

"It's vital that I get all the information I need, young man. Believe me, I do want to talk to you, in time," Deaden said. "If your mother is suffering from the result of her divorce, I think she would be better off coming with us."

"She's fine where she is." Liam raised his voice.

"You're very defensive. Is there something you don't want to share?" Deaden turned her gaze back to Sarah.

However, Liam blocked the captain's view. "Butt out, Cap."

"I warn you, Mister Drake. If I find evidence of abuse in this house, I will not hesitate to clear everyone out and separate you..."

"Go to hell! My mom lied about my dad. That's

why they're not together! It wasn't him at all," Liam shouted.

Deaden's eyes widened, but only slightly. "Really?"

Sarah gripped a nearby pillow. "Yes.... yes, I said some very, very horrible things about Conrad that weren't true." She bowed her head. "Yes, I'm ashamed of a lot of what I said and did. That's what happened."

Liam's skin burned. Watching his mother be humiliated like this drove the metaphorical daggers deeper into his soul. Worse, he was helping to increase her pain. He wanted to defend his father, but in the process, he was hurting his mother.

Before he could rouse another response to their guest, a familiar cry cut through the air, followed by a feminine "Here you go. Someone's a little hungry, aren't they?"

Abruptly, Deaden jumped from her seat. "Is that a baby?"

CHAPTER FIFTEEN

LIAM GLIDED in front of Captain Deaden, blocking her view of the kitchen door. "Yes, it is," he said, slowly, flatly.

"Well, that is fascinating. Yours?" Deaden asked.

"None of your business, Cap, and I strongly suggest we change the subject." Liam was not about to volunteer any more information than he had to.

"Well, that's rather rude, Mister Drake. I came here to talk to everyone possible. I assume that's the child's mother speaking. I think she deserves to hear what I have to say."

Deaden took one long step to the right, out of Liam's path, but the young man swiftly barred her way again.

"Cap, I am warning you to back off and sit down right now," Liam said.

"Liam, stop it!" Sarah jumped from the couch.

"Here, let me go in there and tell Carla what's going on."

But Deaden's eyes locked onto Liam. "You better be careful, Mister Drake. Contrary to what you think, you're not dictating the rules of this game." She nodded her head in the direction of the front door, to the soldiers waiting outside.

"My dad wasted more guys than the goose-stepping thugs you've brought to my door, so bring it on if you feel brave enough," Liam said, quietly.

"Liam, enough!" Sarah seized Liam's right shoulder. "There's no harm in letting her just say hi to Carla. We're all with her."

Any further discussion was interrupted when the door to the kitchen popped open. Carla leaned out, with little Conrad in her arms. "Hi," she said with a smile. "Captain Deaden, right? Everyone's voice is carrying, and I'd thought I'd step in before someone kills somebody."

Deaden's lips curled in a half smile. "Wise decision. You know my name, and I think I know yours now. Carla Drake?"

"Carla Emmet. Not Drake..." She smiled at Liam. "Not yet."

Deaden's smile vanished. "Really? Well that's unfortunate. You seem like a nice woman. Perhaps Liam has certain questions he hasn't yet worked out, but that's not unexpected for men his age."

"Well, I don't know what most men his age are like,

but I do know Liam is just fine for me," Carla said, still smiling, but with a tinge of irritation in her voice. "So, what's your story? Are you coming here to take us away?"

"I'm here to set the stage for your safe relocation, Miss Emmet. Contrary to whatever Conrad Drake has told you, I'm not here to harm anybody. In fact, he seems to have fostered an atmosphere of paranoia and fear. That makes me wonder about how the rest of you are faring."

"I, and my son, and my Liam, are all faring very well," Carla said, "So, I have nothing more to say to you."

"I am curious. Indulge me, please." Deaden took one step closer to Carla. "Why did you and Liam decide to...have a baby?"

Carla narrowed her eyes while keeping her smile. "You might call it a spontaneous act of love."

"In other words, you had passionate sex without thinking about it," Deaden said.

Liam cut back in front of Deaden. "Okay Cap, you're really treading in bad territory."

However, Deaden stepped a little closer to Carla, this time brushing hard against Liam to get by. "Was this before or after the solar EMP hit?"

"Captain!" Liam shouted.

"Really, this is too much," Sarah added.

Carla's smile started to fade. "*Before*, if that's really important."

"Well, that makes you two only slightly less stupid than I would have thought. I mean, bringing a newborn into this world? Rather insane, if you ask me. It's not like you can go down to the grocery for formula and diapers anymore. In fact, if you go to the grocery today, you're probably more likely to be robbed, or shot, or stabbed, or raped..."

"Captain!" Sarah shouted.

"This isn't a place for children anymore, Miss Emmet, not until it's been pacified, and all the dregs of the planet are driven back into their holes, which could take quite a long time. But like I said, you didn't know what was about to happen. So, I trust knowing what you know, that you're not going to make another mistake..."

She stopped talking. Hard metal was suddenly pressed against the side of her head.

"My family is not a mistake." Liam pressed a pistol against Deaden's skull. "Now, you have very, very outlived your welcome here. So, I suggest you and your goons get off my property right now."

Deaden didn't say anything. This time, not even Sarah raised a voice to object to her son's actions. She definitely was backed into a corner.

"Your property? I think the elder Drake runs this place, so I think he decides when my visit is over with," Deaden said.

Loud footsteps drew their attention. Conrad pushed open the hall door, with Camilla behind him holding a shotgun. "Well, I see you got along well with my family, Captain. Though count me shocked you didn't wind up with a gun to your head sooner."

"If you think this is funny, you have a sick sense of humor. Now call your son off so I can continue," Deaden said.

"Call him off? Why would I do that? You heard the man. Get off his property," Conrad said.

"Like I said, if you think this is a joke..." Deaden began.

"It's not a joke. Someday this homestead will be his. He wants to act like the man of the house. Well, I consider it welcome practice. So, if he wants you to go, do as he says, and hit the road. You have no business here, not today and not tomorrow."

Deaden straightened up. "Very well. I can see you're as unreasonable as I thought you would be."

Liam withdrew his gun. Deaden turned and marched toward the front door, with Conrad close behind.

"Word of advice for the future, Captain," Conrad said as Deaden stopped to allow him to open the front door. "Don't insult a lady or her decision to have a child. Both will get your ass in big trouble."

Deaden took a step backward, toward the open doorway. "Sarah tells me you saved her from mobsters in Redmond. If you've seen how terrible it is out there, how can you justify encouraging your son to have babies under your roof?"

"Someone's going to have to pick up this mess after we're dead and gone. Otherwise, we're fighting for nothing," Conrad said.

"Well, I can see you're not fit to make these kinds

of decisions, Mister Drake. I will be back tomorrow. Consider this fair warning." She backed out onto the porch. "Prepare however you like."

Conrad, remaining at the doorway, watched her march across the porch, then down the steps to her waiting men.

————

"DAMMIT!" Liam repeated, his voice growing louder as he retreated toward the den. "Dammit! What was I thinking?"

Conrad followed hot on his tail. "Liam, what's the problem?"

"I could have gotten us all killed," Liam said as he burst into the den. "If I hadn't been so hotheaded, if I didn't draw my gun..."

"You didn't shoot her, son." Conrad emerged into the room, with Camilla and Sarah following. "You did the right thing. Deaden crossed the line big time. You showed her we're not a bunch of doormats, and we don't take shit from anyone. These people will roll right over us if we let them."

Liam leaned against the biggest table in the room. "She got to me. Trash talking me and Carla, going after Mom..."

Conrad glanced at Sarah, who turned her head to the side.

"It was mental manipulation," Camilla said to Conrad. "You were damn right about these people."

"Hey!" Tom barged in. "They're gone. I kept tabs on them until they were out of sight."

Conrad turned around. "And they didn't do anything funny while they were out there?"

Tom shook his head. "They sat, talked a bunch of garbage about the people they've run into so far." He peeled off his coat as he talked. "Didn't really sound like a bunch of good guys to me."

Conrad narrowed his eyes at Tom. "Good to hear. Glad to see these sons of bitches didn't escape your notice." He kept himself from adding, *this time*. Part of him thought chewing out Tom over not noticing possible spies was an error. After all, could Conrad reasonably have expected Tom to pick out well-trained soldiers who accustomed to hiding themselves in the wild?

After placing his coat over his shoulder, Tom approached Sarah. "Hey," he said, "are you alright?"

Sarah folded her arms. "No. Not really."

"Did they do anything to you?" Tom asked.

Sarah pivoted and then walked to the open door. "I...I need some time."

Tom followed her out of the room. "I'll come with you," he said.

Conrad turned to Camilla. The pair exchanged a few looks, knowing what Sarah had been through. Was the woman feeling guilty, hurt, violated for revealing so much?

"So, are we going to throw a party for these guys like we did for Kurt?" Camilla asked.

Conrad placed his right arm onto the table and leaned on it. "Well..." he began.

He didn't complete his sentence. The intense pain that shot up his arm wouldn't allow it.

"Dammit!" Conrad raised his arm and then cradled it tightly.

"Dad!" Liam rushed over to him. "Are you alright?"

Conrad couldn't answer right away. *How the hell did that happen?* Conrad had placed greater strain on his right arm than that, so why did it hurt so much now?

"Guess old age is catching up," Camilla, likely trying to cover for Conrad's unexplained outburst.

"It's...it's nothing too bad. Guess I leaned on it wrong." Conrad wished he had that sling right now.

"That's one hell of a bad lean, Dad. I'll get Doctor Ron," Liam said.

"No. No, the man's busy." Conrad let out a pained breath. "Turns out this thing was hurting me for a while and I asked him to run some tests."

"Really?" Liam asked.

Conrad nodded. This was as much of the truth as he planned to reveal. It would have to do. "Yeah. Don't worry. I'm sure it's nothing, but it always helps to have a doctor under your roof, right?"

Liam nodded. "Yeah. No kidding. Look, if you need anything, just tell me."

"I'll be alright. Hey, why don't you go talk to

Carla? She's a toughie, but she's likely rattled after running into Captain Iron Britches."

"Sure, sure. You're right." Liam turned and hurried from the room.

Not a few seconds after Liam left, Conrad turned and muttered a collection of f-bombs.

"I guess that hit you pretty bad," Camilla said once Conrad had gotten that out of his system.

"Of all times," Conrad whispered, "damn it all. I'm supposed to be getting better, but this thing is flaring up even more lately."

"Maybe it's the damn weather," Camilla said.

"The cold's playing hell on me? Yeah, probably. I had Ron hurry up a test for me. That's why he didn't get to see Captain Deaden. Damn shame. I knew he wanted to talk to her."

"Probably a good thing he didn't," Camilla said.

"Yeah, she's a viper. Trying to drive wedges between us. But you heard her going out, this isn't over." He rubbed his arm. "And I'm in bad shape. God knows I might not be able to get us out of this one."

———

TOM PRESENTED the steaming hot cup of tea to Sarah, who sat on their bed, her head hanging over her lap. "Your favorite," he said gently.

She took it. "Thank you." She sipped. Tom had

prepared the tea while Sarah told him the whole story.

"I'm sorry it didn't work out like you wanted," Tom said.

Sarah sipped again. "Listening to her say my grandbaby was a mistake. It was horrible. But that wasn't the worst of it." She turned to Tom. "Liam said I lied about Conrad, you know, during the divorce. And he was right." She dropped her head against his shoulder. "But it still hurt hearing him say it." Tom slid his hand against Sarah's shoulders. "I know. But it sounded like a real pressure cooker. I'm sure he didn't mean it the way he said it."

Sarah bowed her head. "Tom, I'm afraid my baby hates me."

"I'm sure Liam doesn't."

"You sure?" Sarah raised her head. "You sure he doesn't resent me? Do you think he's ever forgiven me?"

Tom gave his next words some thought. "I know he wants you in his life. I've worked with him. I hear him talk. I've never heard him say a bad thing about you."

Sarah looked down at the cup still in her hand. "I feel like I don't belong anywhere."

Tom wrapped his arm around her. "Baby, you belong anywhere you want to. And don't forget, where you go, I go."

Sarah pulled him closer. "Thanks."

———

CONRAD SHUT his bedroom door with his right arm, which turned out to be a big mistake. Pain shot up his arm once again, and he cried out. "Goddamn it!" *Damn fool*, he thought. *Don't you ever think any more? Stop using that arm so much if it hurts!*

Ron Darber jumped from his seat and reached out to help Conrad, but the rancher drew back like a wounded animal ready to pounce viciously. The doctor instead waited for Conrad to settle down.

"The damn thing's been hell on me," Conrad muttered. "Guess you can get too old to go under the knife."

Darber leaned against the small table. He had holed up in here scrambling to finish up the latest round of tests. The whole table was blanketed with medical tools, including a scalpel and a few glass beakers with solutions. "You may need to go under it again," the doctor said.

Conrad turned to look at his friend. "What?"

"I wrapped up the test a few minutes ago." Darber strung out his words. "You're not going to like it."

"Ron, I've got an army out there ready to storm in here like Attila the Hun, so anything you say probably isn't going to shock me."

"The cancer has gotten into the bone of your right arm," Darber said. "For the moment, it seems to be localized in the radius, but I don't know how long that will last."

Conrad nodded. "I see. Well, I guess that's the end of the game, isn't it?"

"If the cancer hasn't gone any further, and I'm not convinced it has yet, we can try one more thing." Darber sucked in an anguished breath. "Amputating your right arm."

Conrad's stomach suddenly felt sick. He hadn't expected to hear that. Oddly, receiving a death sentence would have been easier than the horrifying thought of being a chopped-up man.

"It could work." Darber cast a glance at his medical tools on the table before continuing. "Of course, the risk is substantially greater. You could die during the surgery, and there's always the risk of infection. And, of course, the recovery period will be much longer and more difficult. You're a strong man for your age, but even you could take a major hit health-wise. Ideally, you would be back on your feet, just learning to adjust with only one arm and hand to work with."

"But I also could be stuck in bed for God knows how long trying to get myself back together." Conrad grimaced. "Well, as much of myself that I still have left. But I wouldn't be able to guard my home like I did before, would I?"

"It'd be very difficult," Darber said. "And there's no guarantee the cancer still wouldn't return. But there's still a chance for you to survive, perhaps for much longer." The doctor smiled a little, as much as he could under the grim circumstances. "Plus, I think your family rather would have a Conrad with one arm than to not have him at all."

"We may not have much of a choice there, Ron. I didn't get a chance to give you the details on our meeting with Captain Deaden, but it didn't turn out well. I don't trust this bunch one damned bit. Tom overheard some bad talk among the soldiers, and our lady captain has a problem with raising new babies in this new world."

Darber nodded. "I hate to bring this up in light of how your talk went, but the ALA might have the resources that can save your life, get you through the surgery and recovery."

"Ron, you know that's a non-starter. I'd be a prisoner, in practice if not officially," Conrad said. Although, silently, he couldn't deny it sounded like an option that would work. "I go with them, it's saying goodbye to this home for good. They probably wouldn't even allow me much freedom."

Darber sighed. "Maybe. But I can't guarantee you anything from this point forward. I run the odds in my head and it's always a coin toss." He shook his head. "I would feel like I'd be killing you if I tried to do it."

"C'mon Ron. I take the risks. You're just the tool."

"Really?" Darber's face tightened. "And if you die, I have to live with that moment every day for the rest of my life. No, Conrad, I'm not a tool. I'm a human being. This doesn't just hurt you if it goes badly. Other people will live with the consequences of what you choose."

"Hey, I didn't mean to put you down like that. I'm just being straight that it's not on you if I don't make it," Conrad said.

Darber gazed at one of the beakers on the table. The small culture inside was likely the one that helped diagnose Conrad's current condition. "I'll do it if you want the surgery. But you must realize things are going to change, whether we want them to or not. As much as you may want, you might not be able to stay here. I know that burns you up inside, but I have to be frank about this."

Conrad gripped the folds of his bedsheets. As much as he despised the thought of it, Darber was correct. "Yeah. Yeah, of course, you have to be. Look, this isn't an easy choice to make, Ron."

"Maybe it'll help if you talk it over with Camilla or Liam."

Conrad sighed. "I'll decide when to tell them."

"Alright. But don't take too long," Darber said. "Time is of the essence."

Conrad rose from the bed. "Don't worry." He smiled. "Whatever I choose, it'll be quick enough."

CHAPTER SIXTEEN

CONRAD STIRRED IN BED. His arm remained in its sling, undisturbed. Camilla snoozed beside him. He envied her ability to fall asleep much easier. Still, having her here filled Conrad with a measure of peace that would have been fully driven out by the news of his health and the ALA.

If this was all about a year ago, if it was just me, it wouldn't matter. I could stand out there and go out in a blaze of glory. But so many depend on me now. Conrad also admitted he had too much to live for now. He didn't feel like dying just yet, but he might be a dead man walking, even if he got through this crisis with the ALA.

As he set his head on the pillow, an odd twinkle caught his eye. He turned to the window. It reminded Conrad of a street light. But that was impossible now. What could it be?

He slipped out of bed and walked to the window.

The light came from the woods beyond his property. The light blinked in a steady sequence.

Conrad knew that signal. He had to go meet with them.

He turned back to the sleeping Camilla. Better to leave her a note before he left. He wouldn't just disappear and leave her wondering what happened if she should awaken before he returned.

———

Conrad's boots crunched the dirt and small branches as he trekked through the woods. He kept the small beam of his flashlight down near the ground, about level with his knees. "Alright, come out wherever you are," he said to the night air.

"Don't worry, we're finished playing hide and seek," spoke a familiar voice.

Conrad shone his light between a gap in the trees. "Who's that? Reginald?" he called.

"It's Reg." The Hooper City resident tromped out of his hiding place and approached Conrad. "Now, you're not forgetting that in your old age."

Then Conrad noticed Nigel, Jeff, Lance and several other men emerging from behind trees. "Well, I've got a lot on my mind." Reg offered his right hand toward Conrad's right hand, but Conrad raised his left. "Easy. Right arm's still giving me trouble."

Reg smiled. "Sorry to hear that." Instead, he lightly slapped Conrad's left arm.

Just then, a face Conrad hadn't seen in a while emerged from behind a tree trunk. Conrad's eyes widened. "Carlos!"

Carlos Almeida waved. "Hello, Conrad."

Conrad approached while offering his left hand. Almeida ran a store in a nearby town, at least until just about all the residents fled shortly after the EMP. "I haven't seen you in ages." Conrad took a gander at the man. He definitely had lost a lot of weight. In fact, Conrad had to study the man's face to be sure it was Carlos Almeida. "In fact, you disappeared months ago. What happened?"

"Quite a story," Carlos said with an awkward smile. "I got sick for a long time. Nearly died. I was brought to Hooper City to get my strength back."

Conrad wondered how much strength Carlos successfully recuperated. Conrad had cashed in eggs and vegetables in his store for years, and the man always wore a bright smile and a head of thick hair. Now age lines cut into his cheeks, and tints of gray appeared on his hair roots.

The crowd continued to grow. Now Conrad counted about twenty-five men and women. "So, what's with all the party guests, Nigel?" Conrad asked. He looked down and noticed the belt on Carlos's waist. He was packing two guns, one resting in a holster on each side of his waist. That was an additional surprise. Conrad never had spotted Carlos with a weapon, either.

"We've come to help you, Conrad," Almeida said.

Nigel stepped close to the old rancher. "We're here to stand with you. The army makes a move, we make them regret it," Nigel said.

Conrad looked at all the men and women behind Nigel. "Well, I'm honored and humbled by the turnout. But it's not your fight."

"Maybe it's time it was," Nigel said. "Conrad, the army isn't far from Hooper City. If we don't stop them at your place, they'll come after us. Hell, they probably already are there. I'd bet my twelve-gauge shotgun that they had spies in my city asking about you."

"If you try fighting them, odds are most of you will die," Conrad said, "and then Hooper City will be easy pickings for whoever's still out there."

"Hooper City's lost either way," Nigel said. "At least out here we can weaken them, maybe show them that pushing onward isn't worth it."

"For the past few months, we've been free to do as we want. Maybe it's not worth it if we must live under someone's thumb," Jeff said.

"There's no way anyone would follow them if they kill you and other innocent people," Carlos added. "Word will spread. People will stand against them."

Conrad hoped that would be true. Even so, he was starting to wonder about Captain Deaden. She might be too authoritarian for his tastes, but was that lady really going to storm in and grab him and his family by force, even if it meant shedding blood? Sure, she wanted his land's crops, but that could be greed talking. Land and resources were a precious commodity. People would lie and cheat to get them.

So why don't I think Joanne Deaden is in that group? Conrad scratched his right cheek. Maybe Sarah's influence was rubbing off on him. *Who'd have guessed that could happen?*

But if she truly wanted to do the right thing, then Conrad had an idea that might just secure his family's future.

"I've got a plan." Conrad smiled. "I think it'll be just the thing to send Captain Deaden and her flunkies packing." His smile then faded. "At least, it may be enough to broker something. But I'll need your help. Won't take much, but did you bring any gasoline with you?"

"We did." Nigel turned to Reg, who nodded and walked off into the crowd. "Not a lot, maybe three cans."

"Two will do," Conrad said.

Nigel took a step closer to Conrad. "What are you going to do?"

Conrad licked his bottom lip. "You played poker recently?"

"I did before all the craziness started. Guess I stopped because I didn't want to fall into bad habits. But I do recall I was pretty good at it."

"Bullshit!" Jeff called from a few steps away.

Conrad chuckled. "Well, I'm a bigger fan of gin rummy, but I've played a few good rounds. With your gas, and some of mine to boot, I think I can put together my own winning hand."

"Now is that a real winning hand or a bluff?" Nigel asked. "Because if it isn't four aces, Captain Deaden might call your hand if she's got something better."

Conrad watched as Reg returned with a single can of gas. "She might. But she might not have a winning hand, either."

————

CONRAD GRIPPED the gas can hard with both hands. *This is goddamn humiliating*, he thought. Unfortunately, he could not trust his right hand to hang on to the can's handle. At least with Lance by his side helping to haul the gas to his home, he didn't feel quite as burned up about it. The young man had been present at the surgery, so he understood Conrad's problems.

He and Lance, who clutched his own can of gas as he walked, tromped slowly through the tall weeds on the way to State Road 22. With the tall trees, they were almost completely enveloped by darkness. Lance had asked to use a flashlight, but Conrad refused. The visit from Deaden had set his nerves on edge, and he hesitated to cast any light, even if he aimed it low. He wondered if she had left patrolmen around to spy on him. Fortunately, he had scouted out the surrounding land dozens of times. He understood how many steps it would take to reach the road, and where the cover was best.

"Ow!" Lance suddenly cried out.

Conrad turned his head. The thick darkness made it impossible to see if Lance had hit anything. "Problem?"

"Damn. Sorry. I hit a sharp twig...no, a tree root," Lance said.

Conrad chuckled. "Yeah, the remnants of a great oak tree that fell about ten years ago. Just keep close behind me. We're almost out of here."

Conrad led Lance to the side of the road. The rancher looked both ways. It seemed like a weird thing to do as no regular traffic had passed through here in months, but Conrad remained concerned about being watched.

There's probably no chance that I can spot any scouts in this darkness, he thought. But on the other hand, they probably couldn't see him either, or at least they wouldn't know what he was holding, unless they scouted the road with night vision goggles.

He couldn't put it off any longer. "Let's go," he said.

Conrad slipped across the asphalt as quickly as he could. With Lance accompanying him, the rancher made it to the other side, near the boundary of his ranch's fence.

"Just keep close," Conrad said as he slowly marched through the grass and weeds. "So far, no one's seen fit to mess with us, but I can't take any chances."

"Right," Lance said.

Conrad laughed. "You don't talk very much, do you? No need to clam up. I don't think we're going to draw bad company just by chattin'. So, where are you from?"

"I grew up in Far Range," Lance said. "Lived there all my life. Not much to talk about, just a tiny town off 22."

"Any brothers? Sisters?" Conrad asked.

"No. Just my mom and dad."

"Ah. Can I ask if they're in Hooper City with ya?"

Lance sighed. "They were vacationing in Florida when the sun fried everything. I haven't heard anything from them since."

Conrad shook his head. "Damn. Sorry to hear that. But it doesn't mean they're dead necessarily."

"I know, but everyone says not to get my hopes up."

At last they had reached the point where the fence curved inward. Conrad turned toward the side of the house. "Now, stay close, because Bertha and Goliath here are guarding my home. We'll have to slip around them to get around back."

"Bertha and Goliath? What...holy shit!" Lance stumbled backward when a big shape suddenly obstructed his path.

Conrad laughed. "See?" He put the gas can down, then rapped the tree trunk with his left knuckle. "Put these two babies here so no one could drive up to my place uninvited." He picked his can back up. "Course, that doesn't mean they can't show up with a tank or a hundred men."

Lance followed Conrad toward the home. "How long have you had this place?" Lance asked.

"Oh, thirty years, give or take. I got it pretty cheap. After the missus decided we were through, I didn't have a ton of cash at my disposal. But it turned out the fella who owned this place really didn't under-stand farming all that well. Once I cleared the land, dug the irrigation, reinsulated the inside and added on the den and the porch, it really started to be something."

"So, you built some of this house yourself?"

"Sure did. I might have to think of adding on some more with my grandson and probably a whole flock of them just behind him."

Lance kept his eye on the house as he walked, despite the fact it looked almost formless in the dark.

Once they had reached Conrad's back porch, the rancher set down his can. "There." He then groaned. "Shit." He stumbled to a nearby chair and sat down. "My right arm's wondering why I'm not in bed like a good old geezer." He massaged his right limb.

Lance placed his own load down next to Conrad's. "Do you need help?"

"Naah. Just a few minutes of rest. I'd offer you something to drink, but it won't be long before morning, and I need my wits about me." He pointed his thumb to a nearby seat. "C'mon, sit down. I'm not going to make you stand around like a statue. Rest."

Lance obeyed. He shifted around in the seat to make himself comfortable. Meanwhile, Conrad let out a sigh and looked at the stars beyond the porch.

Just then, as the moon's light shone on the top of the house's wall, Lance sat up. "What happened there?" He pointed to the spot.

"That?" Conrad turned around. "Just a bullet hit."

"Oh. Is that from when Derrick came after you?"

"No, that's a Kurt Marsh special. I got some mementos around here that I've never fixed. Sometimes they're just painful reminders. It's a hell of a thing when people die on your land."

Lance fidgeted a little, moving his legs back and forth against his chair legs. "I was wondering, did anybody get badly hurt during the fight with Derrick? I know nobody died."

"Well, no one suffered anything lasting, if that's what you mean," Conrad replied.

"That's good. Really good. I was worried."

"Yeah, we made it through alright, though that's when poor Cammie got her first bullet wound. She took one during each of our battles. I joked that if this keeps up, she'll rattle like a jar of change when she walks." He chuckled. "They said you could hear the metal inside Andrew Jackson when he walked by you. He took so many hits in shooting duels, and he never got the bullets out."

Lance nodded. "Did you ever run into the guys that tried to take your place?"

"No. I heard about some of them. Rumor had it some of Kurt's men actually killed a couple of them in a gunfight. Then some others tried to steal the harvest in Hooper City. Don't sound like people I'd ever want to keep tabs on, except if they tried anything funny with me again."

Lance bit his lip. "Right." He cleared his throat. "I'm sure some of them feel pretty stupid about the whole thing. Derrick, he sounded like he could solve everyone's problems. I guess when you've had your own world turned upside down, lost everything, and don't have a clue where your next meal is coming from, you'll do anything. You can even talk yourself into doing something you'd never want to do." A tremor ran through his body. "It's not easy to live with."

As Lance spoke, a growing suspicion came over Conrad. At first, he wondered why Lance was so interested in the gunfight with Derrick. Then, Conrad recalled what Nigel had said about giving sanctuary in Hooper City to one of Derrick's men.

Somehow, it all fell into place. Conrad gripped the chair rest. A flood of angry emotions washed over him, and if his arm wasn't still stinging, he might have said something. Being forced to think cooled him back down again.

Get it together, he thought. *This isn't some psychopath like Kurt. And if he wants to be on the straight and narrow, you'd better make sure he stays that way. At least get a feel on how he's lived since.*

"So, what's life been like for you since summer?" Conrad finally asked.

"Hard. I never thought I'd ever have to work for my own food and water like this. If I jumped in a time machine and went back a few years, my past self wouldn't recognize me." Lance held up his hands. "Nigel, Reg, all the men in Hooper City pushed me to the wall."

"So, you appreciate what it means to work honestly, and not to bite into the bullshit that guys like Derrick throw around to attract knuckleheads?"

"Yeah." Lance ran a hand through his hair. "Yeah, I was a big knucklehead."

Conrad settled back in his chair. "You got a girl?"

"I do. I mean, yeah, I definitely do."

Conrad nearly smiled, but he didn't feel like it just yet. "What's her name?"

"Tracy," Lance replied.

"Far along?"

Lance rubbed his eyes. "Well, after New Year's Eve, I think we are."

Now Conrad smiled. "I had a feeling you might. That's good. Now, I'm not saying you're there yet, but you do realize if you and the lady have a bundle of joy, you're going to have raise him, or her, in a place that's far different from the world you grew up in. No smart phones and Internet and video games. You think you'd be ready for that?"

Lance looked straight into Conrad's eyes. "Well, I wasn't ready for everything around me to go to hell. But it didn't matter. I had to change, or I'd be dead by now. So, whatever happens, I'll work hard to give my family a good life."

Conrad nodded. *This kid sounds like he's had reality pounded into him good and hard. I think he'll be fine.*

Conrad rose from his seat. "You should get going. I've got some things to take care of."

Lance stood up from the chair. "Sure."

Conrad swallowed. "Look, don't feel you owe me anything from this day on. In fact, I'd prefer you keep your distance for a little while. You want to set yourself at ease over the past, then live well, and if you do end up siring your own brood, they're going to be a part of the future of this country. And the fewer knuckleheads we have out there, the better."

"Right." Lance smiled. "Thank you. Thank you very much."

Conrad lightly slapped the side of Lance's right shoulder. "Good, good."

He stood by one of the porch posts as Lance walked off toward the front of the house.

CHAPTER SEVENTEEN

CARLA YAWNED as she rocked little Conrad in her arms. "Someone really needed his midnight snack, didn't he?" The baby didn't respond, instead nesting gently in his mother's embrace. "Yeah, you get to be carried around and sleep, but someday you're going to have to walk on your own two feet!"

Giggling, Carla stepped through the threshold into the living room. To her surprise, Liam, Conrad, Camilla and Sarah all had gathered there. They weren't preparing for the day. They just...stood there.

"Hey." Carla laughed nervously. "What's going on?"

Liam smiled, but the red in his cheeks showed he was hiding something. "Well, we were going to wait to do this, but dad wanted to see if we could go ahead, well, right now." Behind him, Conrad chuckled. The older man leaned a little bit, standing unsteadily, and bags showed under his eyes. Carla wondered if he had had any sleep.

Camilla walked up to Carla. "Here. I'll hold him for you." She extended her hands to little Conrad.

"Okay." Carla slipped her son to Camilla. Little Conrad didn't make any noise, evidently still deep in dreamland. Then, with a wolfish smile, Camilla crept away to the couch, where she sat down.

Liam dug into his pocket. "I, uh, I have something for you. Actually, there's something I want to ask. Damn." He looked to his parents with a pathetic expression. "I'm botching this, aren't I?"

"Just shut up and ask her," Conrad said.

"Right." Liam cleared his throat. "Carla, I want...I want to ask you..." He jabbed his finger into his pocket. "Actually, let me, uh, grab it first."

Conrad turned to Sarah. "You can admit it. He's not really my son, is he?" Sarah responded with a slap to Conrad's chest.

"Ah, got it!" Liam pulled his hand free. Then he opened it up, showing off the ring he had traded for in Hooper City. "If you'll have me, this is for you."

"Oh Liam!" Carla took the ring. "This is amazing. How did you get this?"

"Turns out rings are much easier to get nowadays if you pay in canned food," Liam said with a grin.

Carla put it on her finger. "Perfect." She hugged Liam tightly. "Thank you, thank you."

"Marry me," Liam said.

"Oh, I will," Carla replied, almost dreamily.

Liam pushed Carla back to look in her face. "No, I mean marry me right now."

"What?" Carla laughed.

"I think we should," Liam said.

Carla smiled. "Well, sure, I'd love to do it now. I just thought we'd have some kind of, you know, ceremony. I could at least change out of my pajamas!"

Liam nodded. "I know. But Dad really wanted this as soon as possible. You know how the times are. And I think I've waited far too long for this."

"But who's going to marry us?" Carla asked, "There's not even a priest here."

"I'll do it." Conrad said. "Closest thing to a man of God in this house, after all." Sarah shot him a sarcastic look, while Conrad replied with a good-natured nod.

Liam took Carla's hand. "Ready?"

Carla giggled. "Yeah."

The pair strode up to Conrad. The rancher smiled tiredly as he spoke. "Dearly beloved, we all gather here in the sight of God to unite these two young-sters who as we can see already have united and produced this wonderful baby boy." He gestured to Camilla and little Conrad in her arms. "Well, who am I to judge? It's not like I waited before the honey-moon for your mother—"

"Conrad, I swear..." Sarah said.

Conrad cleared his throat. "Anyway, uh, yeah. It's wonderful you two found each other. And I just want to say I'm very proud of the both of you. So, Liam do you take this lady to be your...what is that word...lawfully?"

"Lawfully wedded wife," Camilla said.

"Oh yeah. Never could remember that part. Lawfully wedded wife, to love and cherish, for all your days, so long as you live?"

Liam turned to Carla. "I do."

Conrad smiled. "And you, Carla, do you take this man..." As he spoke, his eyes drifted toward Camilla. "Take this man to be your husband. To love him, to cherish him, to be by his side through the good times and the bad, in sickness and in health, for as long as you live?"

"I do," Carla said.

But Conrad only saw it out of the corner of his eye. Camilla had mouthed an "I do." Conrad just smiled and nodded.

"Conrad?" Sarah called.

"Oh, right. Well, since I'm the head of this household, and thus the top official here, I pronounce the two of you man and wife." Conrad stepped back.

Carla turned, coiled her hands around Liam's neck, and pulled him close for a kiss.

Sarah clapped. "Whoa, softly," Conrad said, "baby's still sleeping." She quickly softened her claps.

Carla wiped a tear from her eye. "Wow. This isn't quite how I pictured my wedding day, but it's...it's better." She turned to Conrad. "Thank you." She hugged him.

"No problem, darling." Conrad patted her gently with his right hand.

Liam then took hold of his wife by her shoulders. "Let's get dressed. We've got a big day ahead of us." He eyed his father with a worried look. Conrad just nodded back.

———

SARAH LINGERED in the room as Camilla left with little Conrad. "That was beautiful," she said.

"Probably didn't think I could pull it off, huh?" Conrad asked.

Sarah strolled in a semicircle near the door. "You might think I don't give you a lot of credit for things like this, but you do have your moments. Maybe sometimes I don't tell you so. I am curious why you insisted on putting this on, beyond just worrying about the world we live in."

"Like I said, our dear Captain Deaden is planning on paying us another house call. And even if we make it through alright, I'd just as soon make sure we don't have any regrets."

"You sure there's nothing more to this?" Sarah asked.

Conrad smiled. "Nothing you need to worry about."

Sarah folded her arms. "I know there's something. There's always something." She sighed. "And I guess, as always, I'll be the last or the second-to-last person to find out."

Conrad looked at her with sympathy. He realized, feeling guilty, that the two of them were never as close as they had wanted to be. Yet, he still couldn't tell her the whole story of his failing health and what it meant.

He smiled. "You ever heard the story of how Ulysses S. Grant died?"

"Sorry, can't say. I was always more of a math girl than a history buff."

"It's a fascinating story. Never gave it much thought until recently. You know how Grant was a general in the Civil War, then became president. Well, Grant was a man who loved his cigars. Back then, there wasn't all the hubbub about smoking and cancer, so Grant probably didn't figure he was in any trouble. Then one day they found a tumor in his throat. He was a dead man walking. But that wasn't the worst of it. Turns out Grant left his family in one big financial hole. He got swindled out of a lot of his money, and if he died, his family would be stuck in poverty."

"So, he makes a deal to have the great author Mark Twain publish his memoirs. If he could pull it off, he'd leave his family well-off again. But the man's racing against the clock. He can't even lie down anymore. Talking, it was agony. The man knew nothing but pain for those last weeks."

He smiled a little. "But it was worth it. Grant beat

the Reaper by five days. The memoirs took in a lot of money. In today's dollars, it'd be millions. His family was saved from ruin." He turned to look at Sarah. "It's funny. You can picture this man who had survived a war and been president of the country for eight years. Now he's sitting in a chair writing like hell because that's the only thing he can do for his family before he dies." He blew out a small breath. "Well, not every man's story ends like that. Sometimes the ending's a little bigger, a little louder."

Sarah bit her lip. "Well, I guess we don't know how it ends until it's there staring us in the face, don't we?"

"Yeah." Conrad took a good look at Sarah, then turned to the door. "Well, I guess we have to get started."

———

CONRAD PUSHED OPEN the basement door. "Thanks for giving me a hand, Liam," he said as he waited for Liam to pass him by. Conrad followed his son down the steps until they reached the basement interior, which was more like an armory. The only thing more conspicuous than the weaponry was the large shelter taking up half the basement space.

At the moment, the vault door was wide open. Ron Darber already was inside, chatting quietly with Carla, who looked hastily dressed. She was cradling her son, who was playing with one of the rattles Liam had brought back from a prior trip to Hooper City. Tom, Sarah and Camilla were checking weapons by the door.

"So, what's the plan?" Liam slowed his pace by a gun rack on the wall, but Conrad picked up the pace toward the vault door, so Liam followed beside him. "You want to put Carla and the baby in the vault?"

Conrad stopped at the door. "Oh yes, for sure. But she's not going to be alone." At that moment, Sarah, Camilla and Tom all turned to face Liam.

The young man backed up a step. "What you mean?"

Sarah shook her head. "Sweetie, we're all going in. All but your father."

Liam let out a shocked laugh. "Excuse me? You-- you can't be serious."

Conrad put his left hand on his hip. "Sorry, son. This isn't going to be the kind of party you're thinking of. For this one, I've got to be the only guest on the list."

"Dad, you're going out there by yourself?" Liam turned to Camilla, then to Tom. "Did he tell you all this?"

Camilla sighed. "We all got together, and Conrad laid out the choice for us."

"I'm going to meet up with the captain and nego- tiate. I think her little show of force might not be everything she wants to think. But I've got to do this alone. None of you can get caught up in this," Conrad said.

"Dad, you need someone to back you up!" Liam got up close, nearly in his father's face.

Conrad grasped his son by the shoulders. "I'll be fine. Trust me, you're doing much better for me by being safe with your family."

He pulled Liam close and hugged him tight.

Then Conrad let his son go. "C'mon, do this for me." He backed away, stopping to look at Camilla. She nodded at him with a sad expression. Liam's heart quickened when he noticed Camilla's face. Was something else going on?

No, he couldn't leave his father. He turned to give chase as his dad started up the stairs.

"Liam."

The younger Drake turned his head. Carla was calling to him from inside the shelter. His son raised his head in Liam's direction.

A lump formed in his throat. He understood the choice he had to make.

Liam turned and walked toward the shelter door.

———

DEADEN'S BOOTS touched the property of Conrad Drake. She eyed the homestead, wondering what would come next.

"Captain." Gin marched in front of her.

"I know." Deaden backed up a little. Ten soldiers walked past her. "Secure the premises, but do not use deadly force unless you are fired on first."

She waited as Gin led the men directly under his command to the front door. "Captain!" Gin pointed to a sheet of paper taped to the doorframe.

"Bring it to me," Deaden called to him.

Gin tore the page free and hurried back to his commanding officer. Deaden unfolded it and read it aloud. "Come around back alone. Don't worry. Just want a friendly chat. Drinks are available. Conrad."

Matthew, who was part of the company that just had arrived on the property, grimaced. "This guy really thinks he's funny, doesn't he?"

Deaden crumpled the note in her fist. "Probably so, but I don't think this is a trap." She turned to her men. She had brought along thirty soldiers this time, with an additional twenty waiting out past the road. Perhaps Conrad understood the odds were against him and wanted to talk his way out of this situation. "Carry out the operation inside the house. I'll go meet with him as he says."

The soldiers obeyed her commands. Deaden marched around back, down the side of the house, until she reached the back porch.

A bottle of whiskey rested on the table. Conrad stood behind it, glass in hand. "Good morning," he said. "Thought you'd show up a little earlier, but I guess you're not an early riser." He put the glass down on the table. "Care for some whiskey? I'd offer you some of my favorite bourbon, but I polished that off a couple of months ago."

"I don't drink," Deaden said icily.

"Now, you don't drink because what? You don't like the taste or you're, shall we say, morally opposed to it?" Conrad asked.

"I don't drink on the job, Mister Drake. When you're directing dozens of soldiers, sometimes into combat, you can't afford to get yourself drunk."

Conrad poured himself a glass. "I figured you weren't up to it." He quickly took a swig. "To be honest, this is a pretty poor substitute for my favorite bourbon." He exhaled loudly before reaching under the table and picking up a glass bottle of clear liquid. "I filled this with water. If it's more to your liking, I'll pour you some."

"Mister Drake, I am not here to drink with you, and I don't know what you have in mind to talk about. I explained to you that I intend to relocate you and your party to the camp. So, there is nothing more that needs to be said."

"You said all of that." Conrad took another drink. "Doesn't mean I accept it."

"Captain!" Gin walked into view from around the house. "We haven't found anybody in the house. We've checked in all the rooms."

Deaden widened her eyes a little. "Keep searching. Go through every closet and the attic with a fine-tooth comb."

"Sorry, Captain, but this little chat is between you and me. You won't be finding anyone else inside there," Conrad said.

Deaden leaned against the table. "So, what did

you do? Packed them up and sent them away? Rather sick thing to do with a couple with a baby. Think they can survive out there?"

"Maybe I do magic in my spare time and I just made them vanish in my magic suitcase," Conrad said as he poured himself another drink.

Deaden's hand flew around the bottle. She tossed it against the fence, where it shattered. "Enough! I'm through playing games with you! Now, whether you sent your family away or not, I don't care. But this ranch, these fields, they now officially belong to me. So, if you're through guzzling down your drink, you're coming out with me."

"Easy, Captain." Conrad gulped down the last of the whiskey. "You said you needed crops for your refugee camp. Now, there's a good harvest out there waiting. I wouldn't be neighborly if I didn't take you out there and show you around."

Deaden eyed him with intense skepticism.

"Look, I worked those fields for about thirty years. You want to stumble around, wondering what I've planted? Let me give the tour at least, maybe help you take a few for the road."

Deaden backed up a little, her stance relaxing. "Alright."

Conrad gestured to the fields. "After you."

"I think you'll go first," Deaden said.

Conrad put down his glass. "As you wish."

CHAPTER EIGHTEEN

CONRAD STOPPED a few yards from one of his corn-fields. "Wait." He raised his right hand, not caring that doing so provoked additional pain. Captain Deaden halted her approach, stopping about two yards away. "You might not want to get too close to here," he said.

Deaden folded her arms. "Why?" Her frown grew deeper. "For a tour guide, you haven't described much of what's around here." She sniffed the air. "And why do I smell gasoline?"

Chuckling, Conrad pulled out a cigarette lighter. "It's funny. My brothers loved to smoke. Me, never could acquire the taste for it." Then he flicked the lighter, producing a small flame. "Feel like popcorn, Captain?"

Deaden made a fist. "Mister Drake, if this tour doesn't become productive real fast, I'll simply take you into custody and we'll dissect your farm ourselves."

Conrad narrowed his eyes. "That'll be hard when all you got to dissect is a field of ash."

He tossed the lighter into the corn field.

A plume of flame shot from the corn stalks, and then quickly spread out across much of the field. Deaden dashed backward several paces toward the tomato patches. Conrad just stood where he was and chuckled.

"I dowsed everything, my dear. The fields, the ground, even my own house. All this morning, shortly before you and your friends showed up."

Deaden's eyes widened. "You're insane!"

"No, I call it a good negotiating tactic. You want my land and its produce. I can take it away from you and leave you with squat. In fact, I dare say you couldn't escape this land if it all goes up in flames." Conrad pulled out a second lighter. "I'm ready to ignite those beautiful tomatoes behind you."

"And you think you'll escape if you ignite everything around us?" Deaden shouted to him.

"I'm prepared to die here, Captain. This is all or nothing for me. The question is, are you prepared to risk your own life over a single farm's crops?"

Deaden straightened up. Conrad had rattled her. That much was certain. She knew she had betrayed fear and was trying to pull it all back. "You give yourself too much credit. Let this place burn. There are other ranches along this road."

"Really? Sure would be a shame to lose all this, right? You're not fooling me. You know resources are precious and you need food and water quickly. Besides, what would your superior say if you lost all this?"

The fire continued to burn. Conrad cocked his head back. "Well, Captain?" he asked.

———

LIAM FUMED at the closed vault door. "I don't believe this. What's he thinking?" He ran a hand through his hair. "For shit's sake."

Carla boosted little Conrad up closer to her shoulder. "Liam, maybe your dad has a plan."

Liam turned to Sarah. "Mom, what is going on here? What did he tell you?"

"Sweetie, he wants you and Carla and little Conrad to be safe," Sarah replied.

"Believe me, I want to be out there with him," Camilla said. "But he said Deaden shouldn't have any bargaining chips."

"Your father can be quite persuasive," Darber added. "But he believes he can settle our case with Deaden once and for all."

Liam turned away. "But why wouldn't Dad tell me?" His voice sounded much younger for a moment, almost like a child's.

Sarah rose and walked over to him. "I'm sorry we

had to do this. If there was anything we could have done, anything at all, we'd have done it."

"Is there a time lock on the door again?" Liam asked.

"No, since we're all in here, Conrad felt we could unlock it ourselves when we want," Sarah replied.

Tom looked at the door with a grim expression. "This time, he wanted to be sure nobody could get in here, so the door won't unlock by itself. If we have to, we'll stay in here for days, weeks, even months."

Liam shook his head. "I don't believe this." He sat down on the floor and crossed his legs. "How in God's name is he going to pull this off?"

"Hey, we're all worried about him," Carla leaned back. "But we've made it through two disasters already."

Her neck suddenly touched a hard object. "Stay right there," said a male voice, which didn't come from Liam, Tom or Darber.

———

"Captain, you better face it. You don't have the winning hand here," Conrad said, pausing to cough. The smoke wafting through the air was playing hell with his lungs, and he figured Deaden wouldn't last much longer around it either.

"You'd be surprised what I've outlasted, Mister Drake," Deaden said. "And you're a fool if you think this is going to make me back down."

Just then, Gin re-emerged from the house's side door. "Captain!" he shouted, "We have the assets."

Deaden nodded. "What was that about a winning hand, Mister Drake?" She pointed to the homestead. "Here's my cards on the table."

Conrad turned—and could not believe what he was seeing.

Sarah, Ron Darber, Tom, Camilla, Liam and Carla with baby Conrad in her arms were marched out of the home single file, with two skinny men behind them wielding handguns. Gin and a company of seven men surrounded them with rifles. They were trapped.

"What the hell is this?" Conrad asked, his voice raspy, as if he had been punched in the gut. "There's no way in hell you could have captured them." He turned to Deaden. "How?"

The captain chuckled. "What kind of fool did you take me for, Mister Drake? Do you think I'd come charging in here without knowing who I was up against? Days before I even showed up at your door, I had men canvassing your home. We watched your routines, learned when and where you stood watch, and how to get around without being noticed."

"That shelter had a biometric lock on it. That door can stand up to heavy gunfire. You couldn't have broken in even if you knew I had it in my home!" Conrad bellowed.

"Who said I broke in?" Deaden pointed to the two men by Conrad's party. "Meet Hollister and Pi. My infiltration team. They snuck into your home and hid down in the shelter. They were already in there before you placed your family inside."

Conrad trembled. How the hell did he miss this? No, he couldn't have conceived that Deaden would be that on top of him.

"I gave them orders to hide in there for days if they had to," Deaden said. "And no, they didn't have to tell me about the shelter. I knew you'd have something like that built into your house, so I told them what to do ahead of time. I had you nailed the moment I finished talking to you yesterday. You think you're the only rancher I've had to deal with? Someone with their own shelter or panic room? Someone who's erected their own crops, irrigation, everything, and then defends it like it's gold to them?"

Conrad tried his best to compose himself. "It's called freedom, Captain. I don't make any apologies for that, and I dare you to show me where in the U.S. Constitution it says otherwise."

"Please. You built this place because you know the Constitution and every piece of law ever passed by a fatass politician is as worthless as the paper it's written on once law and order goes down the drain. Then it's just gathering together the scraps so that maybe, just maybe, we can put some semblance of civilization back together. Someone has to do that. So, who do you want in charge? Me, or maybe one of those lowlife thugs you've tussled with, like Kurt Marsh?"

"It's not about making the choice, Captain. Freedom's an inherent thing and ought to be protected. You and I can't just go around picking the right overlord to handle it," Conrad replied.

"Well, I'm afraid we're going to have to save all the philosophy for later. As you can see, I have all your family and farmhands in custody. So, I say give this up, and we can talk about distributing your crops and food like civilized people."

"Captain, you're mistaken. Nothing has changed. All these crops are going up in flames unless you work this out with me."

"Mister Drake, I don't think you understand the gravity of your situation. So, I will repeat. Your family is in my custody. They can be imprisoned for as long as I want to, or I can let them all go. You cannot dictate how this goes."

"You're sounding awfully nervous for someone who says they're holding all the cards. Maybe the idea of dying doesn't sound all that appealing to you. Now you want to talk reason? Well, here's some logic for you. Your forces are spread thin, and you can't patrol every corner of this land. Plus, you still need people to work these fields, or you don't get the precious crops you want. You don't need to garrison this place. Let us keep it and work it ourselves."

Deaden paused. Perhaps she wasn't expecting that Conrad would be reasonable, or that she actually would have to negotiate.

"You're right," she said, much calmer than she had

sounded in a while. "I do have bigger fish to fry. Fine."

Then Matthew spoke up. "Captain?"

"He's right, Corporal. I'd just as soon move on. But I have a lot of hungry mouths to feed, so I want half of everything this ranch produces," Deaden said.

"Make it forty percent and we're agreed," Conrad said.

"Dammit, Mister Drake, you're pushing it," Deaden said.

"No, it's assurance. We'll likely have more mouths to feed, and in case you haven't noticed, some of us are getting up there in age," Conrad said.

Deaden glared at Liam, Carla and the others by the house. "It was stupid to have one kid in the midst of this madness and now you plan for more? Forget it."

"Now, as I recall, Captain, we negotiated that ownership of this premises belongs to me and my family. Said ownership includes personal freedom to breed like rabbits if we choose. So, that's not on the table. Now, you get forty percent, but we can make a pretty hefty forty percent, and if we expand the ranch, so to speak, you might just get more out of the bargain."

Deaden stood there, looking almost disgusted. Conrad wondered what else was going in her head. Was she just peeved about raising kids in this blighted world, or was something else nagging her?

Finally, the captain composed herself and said,

"That had better be a generous forty percent, Mister Drake."

"It will be," Conrad replied.

Deaden's posture softened. Perhaps she believed him.

Out of the corner of his eye, Conrad spotted two soldiers, each grasping the ends of a cloth. Rifle handles stuck out. He recognized those weapons. Those were his, stolen from his own basement!

"Hey!" Conrad cried out, "What are you doing with my weapons?"

"We searched your home. You won't be needing those," Deaden said.

Conrad glared at the captain. "And how are you judging that? I fought two gun battles on my property. Stripping me of my weapons is an invitation for disaster."

"My men and I have been pacifying the area. If you're worried about another Kurt Marsh showing up, don't worry," Deaden said.

"Not good enough, Captain. I won't have my family unprotected."

"Mister Drake—" Deaden began.

Conrad raised his lighter. "You forget this? If I don't have any guns, then you'd better be prepared to act as my personal security. Think your men are up for that?"

"Don't be absurd. I can't patrol every dirt road in this state!" Deaden said.

"Then we keep the weapons," Conrad said.

"You have your home and a very generous sixty percent of your produce!" Deaden shouted, "I think you should take what you can get and let it go."

Conrad lit the lighter. "Madame," he said, coldly, "I've lived my life by what I can produce with my hands. And the day I can't do that anymore is the day I take my last breath, and I take it gladly."

CHAPTER NINETEEN

DEADEN LOOKED at Conrad with the wildest eyes he had seen from this lady. "You are absolutely insane," she said. "Do you give a damn about your family? Your son? Your grandchild? Or you just want to go out in a blaze of glory, a martyr for your so-called freedom?"

"Why don't you tell me what you fight for, Captain? Holding guns to a group of simple farmhands? What do you think you're accomplishing?" Conrad asked.

"Sarah!" Deaden called out, "Tell Conrad to give it up! I offer you or anyone in the group asylum. You will have my protection if you want to leave. Just tell him to back off."

Asylum? Conrad's eyes widened. *That didn't sound right. If she's holding them hostage, she ought to point a gun barrel right in their faces and demand they obey her. I might be more right about her than I know.*

"Sarah!" Deaden repeated. "Liam! All of you! These are your lives we're talking about!"

Sarah straightened up, even with the three imposing men pointing their weapons in her direction. "Captain Deaden!" she cried out. "Conrad is our friend. He's our family. He only wants the best. So, I say give him what he wants."

"I second that!" Tom shouted.

"I as well," Darber added.

"We want our land," Liam said, "This is where we want to raise our family. This is our home."

"Captain," Carla said, "I want to stay here. I want to raise my kids. Yes, I want more. I'll do what I need to raise food for others who don't have it as good as I do, but this is the life I want, not one in one of your camps."

Deaden coughed again. "Damn." She returned her gaze to Conrad. "Your family...friends...they don't know where this is going to lead. This is all going to lead to disaster. So...I'll show you."

The captain then pulled out something small. From this distance, it was hard to see. It looked like a pink ribbon, but the bottom half was black, almost like it was charred.

"You want to know what this is? This belonged to a little girl. A couple of months ago, I was in a standoff with a rancher. Same smug attitude. He wouldn't give up anything. I tried to reason with him. He didn't give a damn. Then he, or one of his sons, somebody opened fire on my men. So, we defended

ourselves. We shot back. He used rapid-fire auto-
matic weapons. He used grenades. God knows what
else. And then there was an explosion in the back of
his house." Deaden trembled more than Conrad had
ever seen. "There were five children in there. The
bastard didn't care about them. They, everyone,
everyone in the house burned to death!"

She waved the ribbon around. "That's not the
only fight I've run into, but it was the worst. Hollister, Pi, Sam, some of us have been through hell
together, both in the cities and in the countryside.
I've tussled with scum that enslaved and tortured
innocent people just because there's no police to stop
them. So, if you think I'm impressed one damn bit by
your posturing, you've got another thing coming."

Conrad turned his gaze from the ribbon to Dead-
en's face. In that instant, he realized everything he
had gambled on had paid off. She had been making
mistakes that helped confirm his suspicions, and this
moment just capped it in full.

So, there was no point in continuing the standoff
any longer. He took one final glance at the party by
the house, friends and family all. He would keep that
moment in mind for these final moments.

"Oh Joanne." Conrad smiled, tiredly, but happily.
"Telling me all that was a big mistake." He raised his
lighter high. "You just tipped your hand, and you
were holding nothing but a joker."

He tossed the lighter in Deaden's direction.

The soldiers opened fire.

———

SEVERAL THINGS HAPPENED IN AN INSTANT, the gunfire, the screams from the house, and the lighter zipping toward Deaden. The captain expected to be engulfed in flames from the field just behind her.

But instead, the lighter spun around, over and over, past Deaden's shoulder, until it hit the ground.

But the field did not go up in a blaze. The lighter just smoldered in the grass for a moment before the flame died out.

Deaden gazed down at the lighter. Then she squatted over the grass and sniffed the blades. No gasoline. With all the smoke and gasoline fumes in the air, she couldn't tell unless she was right next to the grass that it wasn't soaked in gasoline.

"He wasn't going to torch his own home after all," she whispered. It was a bluff. He was bluffing this whole time. He likely just soaked that one field just for show. Based on what she had seen of this farm, losing that field was likely a small loss.

She picked up the lighter. Several of her soldiers were rushing toward her from the road, but she wasn't paying attention to them. Instead, she turned toward Conrad's still form in the grass.

Once she approached him, she held out the lighter. His eyes were closed, a look of great serenity over his features. He must have known this was going to happen.

She inhaled deeply. "Looks like you had the

winning hand after all," she said softly, before drop-
ping the lighter onto the grass near his open right
hand.

Five soldiers stood at her side, but she didn't
acknowledge them. Instead, she marched through the
field up to the house. Liam and Carla clutched each
other. Sarah clung to Tom, on the verge of tears.
Camilla and Dr. Ron quaked.

Gin joined Deaden. "Orders, Captain."

"Yeah, guess we take these losers away with us,"
Matthew said, licking his lips.

All of a sudden, Camilla leapt away from the
others, diving right for Matthew and punching him in
the face. "Damn you! You bastards! I'll kill you! I'll
skin you assholes alive!"

"You bitch!" Matthew, regaining his footing,
swung his rifle around.

"Stop!" Deaden shouted. "Arms down!"

At the same time, Sarah grabbed Camilla from
behind and tried pulling her back toward the house.
"Camilla! Stop!" Tom jumped in to help restrain
Camilla.

"Let me go! Just let me die with him, please!"
Camilla shouted with racked sobs.

Deaden tried to remain composed, but even she
had a hard time digesting the death of the man her
soldiers just had killed. Odds are he died before he
even hit the ground.

Then she turned to Liam, his eyes wet, yet he had
not broken down in sobs yet. She spoke directly to

him. "The home is yours," Deaden said. "It'll all be as we agreed."

Matthew rubbed his cheek where Camilla had struck it. "Wait, what are we doing?"

"You heard the Captain," Gin said.

"You're free to live here, come and go as you please, work the fields, just as long as you provide the promised forty percent." Deaden then looked down at the pile of guns and ammunition. "We'll take twenty percent of that, and let you keep the rest. Of course, I get the feeling Mister Drake probably has hidden some more weapons somewhere on this property, but I think I'll just overlook that."

Then Deaden turned to her men. "Alright, pull out. Let these people be." She started walking. "Just let them be."

The group departed. Carla finally collapsed in sobs on Liam's shoulder.

———

LIAM WALKED into the living room through the front door. Each step was jerky. He still wasn't sure this whole hellish experience was not a dream.

Sarah had helped Camilla in first. Camilla refused to go anywhere to mourn alone. She insisted on talking to Liam first, but it was clear she was torn up inside. When she spoke, her voice stammered. "Conrad made a tape. Sound. Audio...audio tape. It's in your room," she said, "You can go...go listen to it."

Liam didn't turn to look at her. He just muttered, "Thanks," and shuffled off down the hall toward his room.

Carla followed Liam, but stopped short of the door threshold. "I think you should listen to it alone," she said.

Liam nodded. He stepped into the room, then shut the door behind him.

The tape player looked old, with its faded paint and worn metal. His dad likely had hidden this way someplace safe, perhaps in a faraday cage, before the solar event occurred.

He almost didn't want to press the play button. It would be the final time he'd hear anything from his dad. But there was no way he could not listen, to not get closure on what just had happened.

Liam pressed the play button.

The voice of his father poured out of the speaker. "Hey, Liam. If you're listening to this, then I bet everything went as I hoped it would." Conrad exhaled softly. "But, as I'm sure, I don't survive. It's alright. Quite frankly, Liam, I wasn't expecting to live past today, and even if I did, my days were numbered far more than you knew."

Dad's days were numbered? Liam leaned a little closer.

"I've got a confession to make. I didn't get Ron just for Carla. I've had some unexplained pains in my arm for a while, and I knew Ron could diagnose it for me. It turned out to be a malignant tumor. That little illness I had? I was recovering from surgery to remove it."

Liam bit his lip. So, that's what happened! No wonder Dad had been in such sorry shape for so long, but surgery? He never would have guessed.

"Ron took out the tumor and a piece of my arm muscle, but that didn't kill the bastard inside me. It migrated into my bone, so we were looking at having my whole arm amputated. I'm sorry, but without a working hospital with working tech, the odds were looking grim. At best, I'd have lingered for a while, but I knew I was a dead man walking."

Liam cringed. Cancer! "Dad, why didn't you tell me?"

"There wasn't anything you or anybody could have done. If I'd have told you, you never would have left my side. Carla and your son need you. Me, I'm done. Shane's got to leave the valley, but at least I left it in better shape."

Liam's eyes welled up. "Dad..."

Conrad loudly sighed before continuing. "I want you to know that having you back in my life has brought me greater joy than I'd felt in ages. This last year has been full of challenges, but I wouldn't have traded it for anything. Seeing the man you've become, the woman you've found, and the grandbaby you've given me, well, what could have topped that? Oh yeah, I got to marry you and Carla, and play Santa Claus for your kid. Damn, this past year was something, wasn't it?"

Conrad chuckled. "I even was able to forgive your mother for the past. In the end, I left this life without any regrets. My house is now yours. Raise your family in it. It's the second-finest thing I ever built. You were the first. I love you, Liam. You, Carla, little Conrad, Camilla, Sarah, all of you. See you around."

The tape went silent.

Liam crumpled to the floor. Then he broke out in sobs. He was barely aware of Carla hurrying into the room to comfort her husband—and to join him in grieving.

———

THE SOUND of thumps drew Liam toward his mother's and Tom's bedroom. He was headed there anyway, to talk to his mom, to find additional comfort, but when he pushed open her door, he discovered his mother putting clothes in a suitcase.

"What are you doing?" Liam asked.

"I'm finding somewhere else to stay," Sarah said.

"You're leaving?" Liam cried, "Why?"

Sarah bowed her head. "I don't deserve to be here." She sounded like she was choking back sobs. "Liam, I took your father away from you. I stole everything you could have had with him. Then you got him back, only to lose him again." She slipped her knuckle into her mouth and bit softly on it.

"Mom, we talked about this. I'm through blaming you."

"Liam, your father is dead. I drove him to this!" She broke from him and dashed to the other side of the bed, by the wall. "This is my fault!"

"And you think he'd have wanted you to leave?" Liam pointed to the door.

"Liam, what am I supposed to do? I can't live with myself." Sarah pointed to the mirror on the dresser. "I see his face everywhere I look! It's like it's here, but I don't know what to say to him!"

"Mom." Liam grabbed Sarah. "I don't want to lose you, too. I want you to stay with me. My son needs his grandma. I need you."

Sarah collapsed in Liam's arms, and sobbed. "Liam!"

"Mom." Liam blinked back tears. "Dad, he would have wanted you to say. He said he forgave you for everything. This house...it's mine, and it's yours to stay in."

Sarah sank her head a little deeper into her son's chest. "Liam...you don't hate me?"

Liam patted his mother's back. "Mom, I never, never hated you."

"Thank you." Sarah relaxed a little. "Thank you for telling me that. I needed to know."

———

LIAM PUSHED OPEN THE DOOR. One lonely soul sat at

the table, but not in the chair where his father frequently sat. Tom sat there, his head hanging over the table. His arm rested there, outstretched, as if he was holding a drink, yet nothing was there.

"Hey," Liam said, "would you like an actual drink?"

Tom looked up at Liam with tired eyes. "I came out here expecting to see your dad. I just realized I'll never be able to talk with him again like we did every night out here."

Liam strolled up to his father's seat. "Well, I guess we'll just have to carry on the tradition without him."

Tom shook his head. "I screwed up," he muttered. "Couldn't keep watch worth a damn. Didn't see those bastards get in the house. Never saw them casing the place."

"They're military. We're lucky they didn't tear the roof off and repel down on cables to get us." He pulled out his father's old chair. "You did the best you could. You shouldn't feel guilty."

Tom let out a loud gasp. "It's going to be a long time before I ever can believe that." He placed his head onto the table. "Me and Sarah, we'll find somewhere else."

"Knock it off," Liam said, "I already told Mom you're staying. That includes both of you."

Tom raised his head. "Are you sure?"

Liam sat in his dad's chair. "Wouldn't have it any other way." He straightened out his dark blue T-shirt.

"Now, how about you go dig us out a drink? Dad's cabinet is still full, and the night is still early."

Tom climbed to his feet. "Sure," he said, "and, thanks."

But suddenly, Liam turned in his chair and called back to Tom. "Hey, I think you should hold off on that." He rose from his seat. "I don't want to go to bed before we've had a chance to prepare a place. For Dad."

Tom paced back to Liam, stopping short of the table. "You have any idea where he should rest?"

Liam turned his head to the farmland beyond the porch. The moonlight washed over an apple tree in the distance, on a hilly ground not far from the apple orchards.

"You know, Dad had a tough life, but I think he still loved his folks and his family a lot. Up there, with Grandpa, I think that'd be the perfect place."

"Need a hand?"

Tom and Liam looked over their shoulders. Camilla approached, her gait a bit shaky, her eyes tired and heavy. "Let me help. There's no way I can think of sleeping until Conrad has been able to rest."

Liam smiled. "Hey. I'm sure my dad would love that."

Before any of them could depart, the side door opened. Sarah, dressed in loose gray jogging attire, stepped outside and joined them. "Could you use another hand?" she asked. "It's the only thing I can do for him now, the only thing to repay him for all the kindness he showed me, all the kindness I didn't deserve."

Liam walked over. "Hey, the more the merrier." Then he hugged her. As he looked over his mother's shoulder, he spotted Carla in the doorway, holding their son in his arms.

"I'd help," Carla said, "I want to."

Patting his mother on the back, Liam replied, "It's alright. You're taking care of his grandson. That will let us finish the work by morning."

Carla nodded while blinking back tears. "Thank you."

Liam parted from his mother to gaze at the assembled party on the patio. "Okay. We'll prepare Dad's resting spot." Then he turned to Tom. "Then, we'll have that drink."

CHAPTER TWENTY

DEADEN WATCHED as the first wave of men closed in on the outskirts of Hooper City. She took a step forward, but then Gin spoke up. "The second unit hasn't moved in yet."

"I know. But I want to proceed in behind the first unit," Deaden said.

"That's never been your style, Captain," Gin said.

"The reports say this city is calm, peaceful, no nuts running the place. I think I'll be fine," Deaden replied.

"All the same," Gin said, walking in front of her, "I'd rather take a bullet before you do."

Deaden almost cracked a smile. "Thanks."

The captain waited until the first unit was about eight paces ahead before hiking down the street. Ten more soldiers surrounded her.

"I'd feel better if we sent along an announcement," Gin said.

"And let these hicks know we're coming?" Matthew asked with a sneer. "Might as well use the element of surprise."

"Halt!" shouted the unit leader up ahead.

"What the hell's going on?" Gin asked.

Deaden stepped out from behind Gin to get a better look. The first unit had come to a stop near a small group of townspeople who had clustered in a semicircle, as if they all were gathered to obscure something. One of them, a balding, middle-aged man, stood in front of them.

"What's going on, Lieutenant?" Gin shouted.

The unit leader turned around. "These guys say they're the town's leaders."

"Leaders?" Deaden started marching toward them.

"Captain!" Gin called after her.

"Bring your asses with me. These are the people I want to talk to," Deaden said.

In a short time, she had joined up with her first unit, forming a crowd of twenty soldiers in all, with more still behind her. The man in front of the group folded his arms as if this was no big deal to him. "You the lady in charge?" he asked.

"Captain Joanne Deaden," Deaden said.

"Nigel Crane. Around here they call me and my friends Councilors of the City," Nigel replied.

"Well, count me impressed that you came out here so quickly to greet us. That makes my job a lot easier," Deaden said.

"What job is that?" Reg asked, standing beside Nigel.

"The distribution of your town's resources to the refugee camps," Gin replied. "Depending on the state of your citizens, we may require you to relocate."

"Our city is fine the way it is," Nigel said. "I assure you, no relocation is necessary. But if you require assistance, we'll be happy to negotiate a fair deal."

"Negotiation? I think you've got the wrong idea about us, hayseed," Matthew said. "We're the men and women in charge. What we say goes."

"Is that a fact, kid?" Nigel asked.

Matthew's nostrils flared. "Hey! Watch it! Nobody calls me 'kid,' and definitely not some country trash like you."

"Mister Crane, I have more than sixty armed soldiers behind me, with even more backing them up," Deaden said quickly to cut in before a commotion broke out. "I am in no mood for bullshitting."

"We're not bullshitting either, Captain." Nigel took a couple of steps forward. "In fact, we're very serious."

A few other men stepped forward, revealing a metal barrel. One of them threw a soaked rag into it, and a fire suddenly rose from inside. Two men then dipped their sticks inside and caught the flame on the tips.

Deaden sniffed the air. It was oil. "Shit!" She and

the rest of the men backed away, with the soldiers pointing their guns at them.

"Like I said, we're very serious," Nigel said as a young man calmly handed the store owner his own torch.

"Are you crazy? What, you're going to throw torches at us?" Matthew pointed his pistol at Nigel's hand. "We can mow you down from six feet away!"

"Oh, these aren't for you. They're for the town," Nigel said calmly.

Deaden walked to look down the street. Other citizens had gathered outside, clutching their own torches.

"Go ahead. Take a little walk. See just how many of us are willing to torch the city before you lay your hands on it," Nigel said.

Deaden stiffened up. "Gin, go get the men and have them fan out into the city. This is purely reconnaissance. Do not, repeat do not open fire unless someone shoots first."

"Captain, I say we take these jokers out now before they do something stupid," Matthew said.

"You have your orders!" Deaden barked.

————

A COUPLE OF HOURS LATER, Deaden's scouts returned with the same stories. No matter what street they explored, they encountered men and women with flaming torches. Even if the soldiers started gunning them down, enough of the residents still could ignite their homes and stores, and there were no immediate sources of water to douse the flames.

"These people are crazy," Matthew said when the final news was delivered. "Do all of these assholes want to burn their own city down?"

"Not crazy. Committed," Nigel said. "I think you get it now, Captain. You can shoot us, kill us, but there'll be enough of us left to start the fire, and it's going to be hell to try stopping it," Nigel said.

"You'd do this just to stop us from helping the people who survived, the people who are starving, the people who are hurt?" Gin shouted.

"We're all on board for that," Nigel said. "What we're not on board for is a military dictatorship. We keep the city and our arms. That, or no deal."

"Oh, screw off!" Matthew said, approaching with a rifle in hand. "Captain, let's take this so-called council into custody."

"Pull back."

Matthew turned, his eyes wide as if he couldn't believe what he was saying. "Captain?"

"I said pull back," Deaden said, slowly and intensely.

Matthew's jaw dropped open. "Again? Again!" He marched up to her, his boots making deep imprints in the dirt. "Captain, this is too much for me! One chickenshit farm is one thing, but a whole town? What do we tell the Colonel?"

Deaden turned to Matthew, her eyes afire. "What

would you have us do? Murder hundreds, maybe more than a thousand people?"

"And if we can't make these people bend, then what good are we?" Matthew asked.

Deaden's hand shook. "We're here to put this land back together. Nothing else matters."

Matthew looked away, his face contorted in disgust. Gin just looked at Deaden, showing both concern and understanding.

But suddenly Matthew snapped. He turned his gun toward Nigel. "Forget it! I didn't come here to play around with these retarded hicks!"

A shot rang out. But it wasn't Matthew's. Matthew never had a chance to fire. Gin shot off one round, clean, and to the chest. Matthew stumbled over and then collapsed face first in the dirt.

Gin straightened up. "I didn't join up with this outfit to put my boot on people's necks."

Deaden turned to her men. Some of them smiled. They agreed with Deaden and Gin. A few of the others shrank back or stood around stone-faced. Even if there was disagreement, it seemed clear no one was about to mutiny to support it.

However, that didn't mean Deaden was going to pull the plug on this mission. She turned back to Nigel. "I still have sick and starving people to take care of. I won't take your city, but I can't walk away with nothing."

"We have good, strong people in this city," Nigel said. "How about forty-five percent?"

Deaden nodded. "From a city this size, I can accept that."

Nigel then nodded. A teenage boy ran up with a box of canned goods. "Here's our token of good will. You can take that and some more back with you today."

"So, you didn't just have torches to greet us?" Gin asked, sounding a little amused.

Nigel drew in a long breath before answering. "We hoped for the best, but got ready for the worst."

Deaden directed one of her men to take the package. "You remind me of somebody I once met."

"Really?" Nigel asked, "What was this person like?"

"Stubborn, pigheaded," Deaden said, "and somebody that'd do anything for his friends."

"Maybe I've met him," Nigel said as Deaden's soldiers gathered the packages.

Deaden nodded. "Yeah."

Once the army had secured the load from the city, Deaden directed them to pull out, but warned Nigel an emissary would appear regularly to collect supplies. "Oh, I forgot. What's the name of this city?" Deaden asked.

"Liberty," Nigel said.

One of the soldiers frowned. "I thought the sign on the road said, 'Hooper City.'"

Nigel chuckled softly. "So it does. Funny, huh? Guess we should get around to changing that."

Deaden's lips curved upward, forming a slight

smile. "We'll take your contributions now, and we'll be off."

———

REG WATCHED the last of the troops leave. "You know, we're never going to be fully out from under their thumb. This still leaves us with one of their hooks in us."

"It was either that, or we all die," Jeff said. "We probably came out with the best deal we could."

Nigel nodded. He kept his gaze on the departing soldiers. "I wonder what he'd think of our little stunt."

Jeff looked at Nigel. "So, Liberty?"

Nigel smiled. "Thought we should make a statement."

———

LIAM LOOKED UP. The apple tree never looked fuller. He almost laughed. The tree looked thin and gloomy the first time he had laid eyes on it. But eighteen years later, the tree's branches had grown out so much it had become the pride of the farm.

Makes sense, Liam thought. *Everything Dad had done around here has prospered. Why shouldn't this tree?*

He turned to watch the crowd approach the tree. His own family had arrived just a few minutes ago, and soon the rest of the household would gather in celebration. "Alright. Let's get ready to wish your grandpa a happy seventy-eighth birthday."

Little Conrad scratched the back of his neck, just below his thick dark hair. The teenager was tall—so much that he overshot his dad and had to step back a little to keep from having a branch smack him in the head. He turned his gaze to the ground just under the apple tree.

A younger teenager, about fifteen years of age, looked at his mom behind him. "Is Grandma Camilla making cookie cake again this year?"

Carla brushed back her long brown hair. It was kept together by the braids, courtesy of the two ten-year-old girls beside her. "Definitely. I made sure she remembered."

"Grandma Sarah's a better cook," said the thir-teen-year-old boy seated on the grass. Then he laughed.

Carla leaned over him. "Riley, don't let Grandma Camilla hear you say that, young man."

"Don't let me hear what?" Camilla asked as she climbed up the hill. Tom walked beside her, with Sarah on his other side.

"Is someone talking bad about my cooking?" As she approached, she narrowed her eyes at the teenager. "Careful young man, because I hear that somebody's finally been able to make some ice cream." She grinned. "And I know who it is, and if you aren't nice, you don't get any." Then she playfully flicked Riley's nose.

"Who's got ice cream?" James asked, scratching the side of his short light brown hair.

"She's talking about Lance," Sarah replied.

"You know that working freezer? Last year they were able to make some ice cream with it," Tom said. "Now, we can't broadcast this everywhere because the poor guy's going to get mobbed."

"I've never had ice cream before," said one of the girls, who straightened out her long red skirt as she spoke.

"Well, Bonnie, ice cream is something very cold and very tasty." Sarah squatted down next to her. "And it comes in different flavors. You get strawberry or chocolate or vanilla..."

"And your head can explode if you eat too much of it," Tom added.

"Really?" James asked.

Riley laughed. "He's lying."

Tom ran a hand through his now fully silver hair. "Well, my head felt that way back in college when I overdosed on too much chocolate swirl."

As Tom chatted with the kids, Liam thought about how much had changed after his dad had passed. In the years since, Liam and Carla had had more children—James, Riley, and twin girls, Michelle and Bonnie. Carla then called it quits, saying she was done squeezing out "bundles of love" as she called them.

Liam looked over at Camilla and his mother. Both women sported fully gray hair, though to Liam's surprise, Camilla had aged faster than his mother. She had carried the burden of helping his father during his cancer surgery and recovery, and was the only one out of the household who knew how dire his father's condition had become. Conrad had entrusted her with perhaps more than anyone else in his life. As far as Camilla was concerned, the two of them were indeed married in heart, even if they had never taken formal vows verbally.

Sadly, a piece of Camilla had died along with Conrad. Even though Liam saw Camilla smile many more times afterward, he never saw the blazing fire in her eyes again. She devoted herself to being a doting grandmother to Liam's kids, but she never tried to pursue love again.

Liam glanced down at his father's gravestone under the tree, then to the dirt next to it. Camilla wanted to be buried there. Liam readily agreed. *But,* as he often told her, *don't drive yourself to an early grave.* Camilla would nod silently and sadly, but the sight of one of Liam's children quickly would brighten her mood. She seemed now to live for them.

Captain Deaden had proved true to her word. The ALA permitted them to stay at the homestead and work the land, provided they turned over forty percent of their overall produce, dairy and livestock to the army. Additionally, the ranch never was menaced by bandits or madmen. Liam and Carla raised their children in peace.

Even so, the years were not without sacrifice, and

even loss. One man would not be here today. Ronald Darber had found happiness with his girlfriend Tara, who reunited with the doctor while he visited Captain Deaden's refugee camp. The doctor never forgot his professional duty, and worked hard for the survivors in Deaden's care. But the years and hard work had caught up with him, and last year he had passed after a serious illness.

Liam looked up at the sky. News about the outside world was picking up again. Rumors abounded that some kind of government was reemerging, this time in the South. Was it benevolent or oppressive? No one could be entirely sure. It was simply another challenge of this new world.

"We got more visitors!" Tom pointed to the house. Lance Wilkins with his wife Tracy and three kids were rushing across the field to join them.

Liam blinked his eyes. *So, he has three now? Oh yeah, you were in town when his daughter was born.* To his surprise, she was tall, coming up to Lance's upper chest. *Damn, time really is passing by.*

But the Wilkins family wasn't alone. Nigel Crane, along with a small party, approached the hill as well. It was likely the whole group, Lance and his family included, journeyed from Hooper City.

"Hello!" Nigel called as he approached. The retired town leader walked much more slowly, with his almost total baldness evidencing his advancing age. Jeff and Reg, also with gray in their hair, followed close behind.

"Well, I didn't expect this kind of turnout!" Liam reached out and took Nigel's hand when he got close.

Nigel nodded. "Well, we're all getting up there. Nowadays when we're not working, we're trying to keep in touch with family and friends."

"So, how is the new council going?" Liam asked.

"Excited." Nigel shook his head. "Three years to build those solar panels and the new wiring across town, and they think they can bring back cable television."

Reg poked Lance in the ribs. "I'll just settle for some of this man's ice cream." Lance chuckled.

Liam did a quick count of the crowd around the tree. It had grown to almost thirty. Would more show up?

"I also had something special I wanted to bring along." Nigel held out his hand. Jeff took the cue and handed him a glass bottle.

Liam read the label. It was a bottle of Texas bourbon. "It's dad's favorite," Liam said softly. The brand was exactly the same as the bottle from which his dad had drank eighteen years ago.

"Took me years to find another bottle," Nigel said. "Damn shame I couldn't get this to him when he still was living."

Lance offered Liam a glass. Nigel popped the cork, then poured a drink for Liam before pouring one for himself. Jeff quickly poured another glass for Tom, who waited with an outstretched hand.

Nigel and Tom clinked their glasses against

Liam's. "To a good friend, and a magnificent father," Nigel said.

"To the craziest son of a bitch I ever met," Tom added. "To the man who changed my life in ways I'll never be able to count."

Liam smiled. "To Dad." He was about to put the drink to his lips, but he noticed Nigel wasn't drinking. Tom also stopped before his mouth touched the glass.

Nigel seemed to read the unspoken question in the two men's minds and explained, "I figured the old man should have the first drink."

Liam nodded. "He always did."

The three men then tipped their glasses and poured their drinks onto the grass in the shadow of Conrad's grave.

———